BYGONES

Also By Rory Haymont

Short Novels

The Girlfriend Experience

Reaper

The Blue Groper

Proximity

The Reputation

Short Stories

Clean

Holes

The Hostel

Death Row

Sheds

Crayons

The Dog's Dream

Revenge of the Geriatrics

The Art Piece

The Last Embrace

The Donation

Bottom Feeders

Run

Russell Hansen was talking into the handset in an angry tone. For Reece this was not unusual. It was the way her parents usually communicated. Occasionally it escalated to shouting, though this was usually mercifully short lived. While this was happening an old pick up arrived on the tarmac and a man who looked like he had just walked off a ranch got out. He stood at the door and shared a few words and a laugh with the driver, pulled out a tired backpack and walked towards her.

The conversation Hansen was having on the phone escalated briefly to nasty recriminations. His voice then moderated to bitterness and devolved to disappointment. The content of the conversation indicating that at least his wife's failure to prioritise the family were consistent behaviours. Hansen's voice embraced martyrdom to impart. 'I try to do something for the family. You've been saying we should be doing more together. And this is how you react.'

Great way to start a holiday. Thought Reece.

He was impatient while there was a response that didn't fit his narrative. The response being she would get a midnight flight the next day. Hence what he had been told needed to be adjusted to realign with the reality he wanted to impose on reality. 'That's the day after tomorrow.'

'We both know it's going to turn into at least four days. You might as well not come at all.' He hung up without bringing the exchange to a close with any opportunity for clarifications or even a little retaliation from the other party. Russell had announced there was to be a family holiday only four days in advance. He had not bothered to enquire about existing plans. Or at least had appeared not to. He could see nothing of importance going on his daughter's life. Though he already knew Tammy had a major event to manage the day after they were to fly down to San Diego. When she reminded him about this he'd suggested she make the family a priority for once and; 'Get someone else to do it'. He appeared to presume one of the biggest events in her calendar was something anyone in the agency could pick up on short notice.

What had caught his wife and daughter out was that this kind of pronouncement had never been made before. They had no inkling it had been triggered, less by a long-term aspiration to visit Sea World with the family, but a profound realisation stemming from developments in his business which had rolled through his conception of what passed for a personal life.

He had been standing a long distance away. However most of the conversation carried to the two people near the plane. As did the noise when he kicked over a trash can after a pause in which his jaw muscles tightened briefly. He had assumed his wife would come.

Reece had been standing all the while leaning up against the plane with her headphones on, eyes closed. Nodding her head very slightly to music that wasn't playing. The technology wasn't turned on. She always listened to the interactions between her parents this way, and then gave no indication she had heard them. She found out what was going on in the family and was content to allow her parents to feel at liberty to be what, in her view, they were. Unpleasant people. This supported her preferred narrative with respect to her life. She had under two years left of this phase of it. Her primary objective was to fly under the radar of their disapprobation while carefully preparing for the next phase which, contrary to every appearance, she was looking forward to, and optimistic about. However anticipating better days to come was unlikely to be a stimulant for harmony in the filial relationships. Reece was much more strategic in life than anyone would have suspected. She could be a good friend. But also expedient and even mercenary.

And in the rare event someone wanted to be nasty, she would respond enough for them to realise that she was way better at nasty than they were ever going to be. Even though it wasn't core to her nature.

Sixteen and seventy-eight days. She had a calendar hung behind the clothes in her wardrobe where she crossed off the days until she could leave. She never missed a day making a mark. She also spent time investigating options that could allow her to leave earlier and live somewhere she would prefer. She'd even considered asking to go and live at her uncle's ranch. But it was too far from a school and her father did a poor job at pretending to even tolerate the man. Jake was the only person that could be considered extended family. And he wasn't even an uncle, rather some variety of cousin on her mother's side. His visits were sporadic. He treated Reece like a person. An ordinary kid. A lifeform he had remarkably few prejudices about for one his age. In more recent times he'd migrated to treating her like he did everyone else. Pleasant. Interested in what they had to say. Though he was retiring if there were too many people in one place or he didn't know the people in any size group.

Reece hadn't looked across when he arrived even though she heard him pull up and say goodbye to the person who'd driven him three hundred miles to be there.

She'd been pretending to be absorbed in music. However she wanted to say hello to the rancher before her father got back. Meanwhile Hansen was a man who found untidiness confronting so had to right the trash can and restore its contents. The way his mind worked, this irritating necessity was absolutely and completely laid at the feet of his wife She might as well have kicked it over herself.

Reece took one earphone off and said. 'Cowboy.' And gave him a nod and a smile.

'Reece.' He replied in kind. That was as far as their greeting would go. Jake Witherspoon had been advised one day by Russell that he didn't like people 'outside the family' giving Reece a hug. Jake had already caused considerable upset. When she was learning to talk, she had called herself 'Reece' instead of Theresa which she found difficult to say. He had been there on one of his occasional visits. Passing through for some reason. He called her Reece a few times, laughing, and so she laughed. From that day on she would refer to herself as nothing else and answer to nothing else. It was a long time before Jake was able to 'pass through' her life again.

He'd placed his bag at his feet and stood patiently. The main thing occupying his mind being an analysis that he should have anticipated Tammy's reaction to her husband's plan.

Part of him wished he'd foreseen this and flown down to San Diego with her. Though it would have been better to make his own way. Either would have been better than fly with Russell. Reflecting a little more though, he realised that would have left the teenager alone with Hansen.

He got few opportunities to visit Reece, and had no other relatives left after the pandemic, a car accident followed by a suicide. Not many people knew he had a degree in Biology. He had taken on the family Ranch halfway into his PhD when multiple tragedies stuck in short succession. It gave him somewhere to retreat to during a difficult time which he didn't manage as well as he wished he had. He did gradually realise that the lifestyle of a rancher suited him well.

Like Reece, he planned put up with Russell in close proximity until they got there. Each had a hotel room. Reece had made the non-sharing of a hotel room with a parent a condition of coming.

This had solicited one of several observations from Russell that he was trying to do something positive for the family and it would be nice if the rest of it could get on board.

It was non-negotiable for Reece. Private space was essential. She already minimised interaction time with her parents, most particularly when they were together. Her bedroom was sacrosanct. As would be her hotel room.

Her father was someone who, even if shouting and petulant a moment before could turn on a cringe inducing false bon homie apparently believing this restored relations. Using the headphone ploy, Reece would invariably respond with a similar, and though brief and equally insincere cheery acknowledgement and wonder that her father never saw sarcasm for what it was. Hence he approached smiling and looking at the two people standing next to the tail of his Cessna Grand Caravan, Reece leaning on the fuselage which he had mentioned a few times he would rather she did not do. She was still a teenager.

He came hands clasped before him to say. 'Flight path cleared. I have a couple of checks. California here we come.'

She appeared to be all unawares of the phone altercation moments before. She thought it would be interesting to see how he answered a simple question. 'Where's mom.'

The manufactured sunny mood was interrupted by an equally manufactured cloud of disappointment. 'Your mother has indicated she might be joining us later, but she probably won't be able to make it.' He smiled as if he had reluctantly aligned with her decision.

'You know how it is with her. Work always comes first.' Reece let the stratospheric hypocrisy of such a statement amble past. Her father's self-delusion was his problem. He also didn't seem to comprehend that people communicated with each other in a world which existed independent from his and the narrow perspective that informed it. When the holiday was announced she had pre-emptively contacted her mother acknowledging she knew the biggest event she was managing that year on the first day of the holiday. Reece said she would be more than understanding if her mother came a bit later. And that she was annoyed that her mother had been put in that position and had felt an obligation, partly on her daughter's behalf, to choose. This was an occasion when Reece's position aligned with what she thought was right.

However her mother could hear the subtle cue warning her not to use her observation as a pawn in parental game playing. If her parents ever tried to integrate her into one of their spats the gloves came off and they were left bruised and on one occasion figuratively bloodied by her analysis. And unlike them. It barely touched her emotions. They could only observe that as breathtakingly harsh as her analysis might occasionally be, it left not the slightest residue of awkwardness, and she returned to her usual occupations untroubled.

Reece knew her father brought out the less desirable traits in her mother. She wondered if her mother was someone who mirrored those she was with. At her workplace she was different. And at the tennis club she devoted an inordinate amount of time to as a committee member she was different again. However purely because her mother had the potential to be a better person didn't change Reece's approach. The teenager sometimes wondered if she was unsympathetic by nature, however she judged everyone with the same measure. If her mother wasn't happy, she should leave. It's not like Reece's opinion of her father was in doubt.

For her part, Tammy might have, with no small dissatisfaction from her employer, handed off the event to a colleague. However, part of her decision to fail to comply fully to her husband's arrangement was to avoid being in a light aircraft with him for six hours, and by doing so probably see the holiday unravel badly before they even arrived in San Diego. Especially when he discovered that she too, had booked a room for herself.

Even with this full complement of background information, when her father gave his answer she simply smiled and replied. 'Okay Dad.'

He went off to complete whatever pilot duties he needed to attend to. In this case some out of the ordinary.

She suspected her father would call his mother when they landed. Stimulate a blazing row and tell her she should not bother coming. This would both take away the opportunity for some pleasant times she might have spent with Reece and Jake and intercut the satisfaction she would get from running a large and complex event and seeing a good outcome for those she delivers it for.

Once Russell was out of earshot Reece said. 'Ready to fly Cowboy.' The hiatus on visits after the 'Reece' incident lasted four years.

On that next visit he had been christened 'Cowboy' because of the hat he routinely wore when outside and the fact he usually dressed in clothes typical of a rancher. He dressed like that because they were the only clothes he had.

'I sure am.' He replied.

'So what did you get me?'

Jake smiled. Had never missed a birthday. Though he always got her things a little different than the normal 'age appropriate' gifts for a girl her parents did. One had been a backpack halfway between a day pack and a rucksack.

Which she always used for school, and had her things packed into it for this trip. This meant leaving behind the matching luggage set she'd been given two birthdays earlier by her father. She'd received a divers watch, and a voucher to a shoe store that resulted in brown Doc Martins which were well worn now.

Jake always got sent a card. It was one that she made from scratch with all kinds of different paper and pictures cut out of magazines or some that she drew. No one else in her orbit got cards like that Another thing that didn't go unnoticed by Hansen. She was otherwise rather unsentimental about 'the days'.

This was her catchall term for birthdays, Mother's and Father's Day and Christmas and new Year's Day and the rest. Her parents found it hard not to notice that her efforts scaped the threshold of what she considered obligatory.

She was initially a little surprised when nothing arrived for her sixteenth other than a card. However there was a cryptic message suggesting he would be passing by sometime soon. He had wanted to be there on the day. However after initially being invited, Tammy advised him in a text from Russell it was a special holiday for 'immediate family only'.

Once he knew this, Jake planned to make an unauthorised visit, possibly to Reece's school to give it to her, though this might lead to a hiatus for any visits until she was eighteen. Jake looked around to see Russell's whereabouts. 'I was going to give this to you when I got the opportunity to be…'

'Not hassled all the time…' Jake's presents were something she anticipated hence she made the enquiry at a time one wouldn't usually choose for present giving. His presents had suggested opportunities to be individual. To feel and behave like a more mature person than anyone else treated her as and had a hint of travel and the outdoors.

Both of which she aspired to enjoy more of in around twenty-one months.

Jake had never had a bad word to say about her parents, and she usually didn't put him in a position where he might feedback obliged to make an observation. He pulled out something wrapped in a soft square of leather. Unfolding the buckskin it revealed a knife. It was a beautiful hunting knife. Old. She knew next to nothing about knives however it wasn't hard to see this was something of high quality.

'You're sixteen now. Every adult should have at least one good hunting knife is my belief.'

She loved the knife and was most pleased with the message the knife was there to confer. She was an adult now. Also that she was first and foremast a person in Jake's eyes. Whether she was female didn't change the fact she needed a hunting knife. It was almost the reverse message she got at home and at school where she was apparently culturally too young to be treated as an adult though she treated adults as equals which was not always welcome. She was not particularly feminine yet disinterested in debates about gender. Reece didn't care.

She had to fight with a metabolism that that didn't subscribe modern western ideal of the female body type many did. She maintained a small, eclectic group of friends and was close to several teachers who taught her about life in addition to the subjects she enrolled in.

'Maybe I'll come out to that ranch I've never been to, and you can help me learn chase animals, kill them, skin them and eat them.'

'Sure. That'll be like every other day at work for me.' She had never been invited personally and when Jake made some approaches to her parents he was not surprised at the response. He turned to look her in the eye. 'Gotta remember to thank those animals when you kill them though.'

'Might sound sentimental but they give up their lives so we can eat. It's the least we can do.'

'Darn. I was hoping to run down and kill a wolf. Does that mean I have to say thanks then eat it.'

'Hah. I wish you could run one down. No need to kill it though. Wolves haven't been seen on that place in a hundred years maybe. I believe their moving down from the north. I wouldn't mind. A beautiful animal. Didn't realise you'd like to do some hunting. Now I know that I'll get you a rifle next year.'

'I'm going to hold you to that.'

'They make some great replicas these days.'

'I'll wait a year longer, then I'll drive over there myself with my rifle and you can teach me to shoot.' They exchanged a glance that had happened occasionally in the past. They were both looking forward to when she could do that.

'I'll be there waiting.' He said quietly

Times like this reenforced a mindset which she had cultivated that she was living with some objectionable flatmates, a remedy for which she would contrive as soon as she could.

They saw someone whose response to their dysfunctional marriage was to develop a heartfelt disinterest in them. When they unwisely decided to attempt to be intrusive they could only stand by and watch as their interventions barely touched on her inner life. They had to give her some credit for the fact that to achieve this level of disengagement, there was virtually never had a valid reason to tell her to do something or criticise her. For her age she was exceptionally diligent housemate, getting most of the housework done while they were both working long hours. Hence she could retreat to her room, the house clean, dinner made or started and be 'very busy with homework'.

On those occasions one or other deemed the exercise of parental power essential and meted out 'consequences' if she judged their case had no merit she blithely accepted the punishment and reduced, for a time, the small rituals of affection the family maintained. However Reece's maturity was real. If a parent provided some observation which, on reflection had merit, she'd adopt the change. This was partly because it was consistent with some of the old books on philosophy Jake sent her. However it was also consistent with her objective of giving her parents nothing substantive to purchase on.

So strategic was she to facilitate her disengagement, she even constrained her social life. They would never guess that rather than giving them the opportunity to limit the exercise of her free will concerning the ability to leave the home, she would wait until complaints were made regarding her failure to make friends and get out of the house. Hence, when getting out was very important to her, it could never be used as a bargaining chip, and she could never be disempowered on that front.

'Time to climb aboard. I'm advised conditions will be good, even a tailwind, though we may have to skirt round a low-pressure system hanging around San Francisco.

Flight time to San Diego will be about six hours and it's going to be a lot warmer than it is here. Hah. You can leave your jackets in the hanger if you want.'

'Great.' Said Reece. She used as few words, indeed as few syllables, as possible because they might create something to respond to. But those she chose were delivered in an upbeat tone and with a smile. She didn't convey a sense of being surly, angst ridden or taciturn. She often said was effectively 'no' in such a positive way people didn't realise she'd chosen to disagree or disregard what they'd said. Russell knew her jacket, last year's gift from Cowboy, was going nowhere.

She suspected her father was looking to expand his business into Southern California. She didn't begrudge him this. It would further reduce their interactions. They boarded a Cessna Caravan. It was modified for rough landing strips because her father too clients hunting and fishing which Reece believed was probably the primary reason for the core client base he could sustain. She knew he didn't especially like hunting or fishing however wanted to have a corporate box at sports games less.

He was also a man quickly irritated by the processes and interactions with the public required in mainstream travel through airport terminals, using rental cars and hotels.

So he flew his own plane, which supported his desire for prestige and arranged limousines to meet him at the hangar or light aircraft departure building and take him to high end hotels. This impressed clients but not his wife. His business was not in the league to sustain those kinds of costs and margins were slim. She was unaware that slim would be a significant overstatement. Tammy had gone back to work when Reece was three to help support the family while Russell 'Grew the business'. This hadn't helped in winning the child's affections because luck ran against her with the quality of carers and the character of children she was left with in the daycare lottery.

It had reenforced an aloofness and a capacity and willingness to retaliate, sometimes a little disproportionately, when those being cared for got nasty. And on one occasion it was a carer who was not good person. The complaints that had come back about her behaviour only taught her she needed to retaliate with greater finesse. Reece's mind had been set on this response to life from an early age. She wasn't the one to start something. She was the finisher. Yet if not placed in that dynamic, away from her parents and with friends it was hard to find someone more relaxed and pleasant.

The two passengers were in the lounge section of the plane when Russell surprised them by going to refrigerator and bringing out a bottle of sparkling wine and getting some fluted glasses. 'Here's to good trip and many more like it.'

Reece was allowed wine at home on rare occasions considered special by her parents. They assumed she drank with friends when she was out. However, her friends weren't into drugs, alcohol nor any of the various nicotine delivery systems because her friends, like her, preferred to read, play video games and made a reasonable effort at their studies. And that wasn't as unusual as many parents thought.

Jake hadn't had a drink in fifteen years and wasn't inclined to start now. It was all or nothing for him. Russell knew this. The two passengers glanced at each other. Reece was about to ask what else was on offer because she didn't like sparkling wine. Russell had a bottle of soft drink if they really didn't want the wine. Provided they made a toast to the start of a 'great holiday at last'. Jake was appreciative that he'd been asked along. He decided he could handle one drink with a man who, to the extent he had the capacity to do so, appeared to be making an effort. They drank while Russell talked about plans for the week.

There was the predictable list of places for people who had never been to that city. Reece was a little surprised that he planned to spend most of the time with them.

'I'll get this girl warmed up. Once you're done Reece how about you come up front for a while. I'll show you what's involved in taking off and if you want to, you can take the controls once we reach cruising altitude.'

'I'm okay.' Reece had learned to smile enthusiastically and even nod as if she'd said yes when she was saying no. It was hard to get annoyed at a girl who was so pleasant to people when she delivered a message that sometimes boiled down to 'get lost'.

In a plane together was one thing. Sitting next to him was another. Russell's recent method of endeavouring to reestablish his flagging parenthood was to, in effect, lecture her with respect to what success looked like and how she, from her current situation, could achieve it. He made little effort to hide his assessment that she was starting from a low base. Such nuggets of wisdom as 'scientific studies have proven that slimmer women are on average more successful' demonstrated how disconnected his counsel was from anything she might respect or take an interest in.

She would be pummelled with a monologue sprinkled with examples of how he had ascended from 'very difficult circumstances' to be flying his own 'corporate aircraft', entertaining clients who had enjoyed 'every advantage'. It was times like this it was difficult to maintain her position below the radar when she had to restrain herself from telling him what she really thought.

'Come on Reece. I want to show you a bit about flying a plane. You may not be interested but you can't tell if you've never tried. You're sixteen now and so you can take lessons if you like. Even if you never use it, having a pilot's licence looks good on a CV.'

This was more specific fatherly interest than she felt it would be fair to say no to.

She chided herself that many people would be grateful to be given the opportunity to fly a light plane, unaffordable though it was.

'Sure dad.' She threw in a belated. 'Thanks.' It turned out every one of her assumptions about his motivations for the trip, and the reason he was especially angry at his wife's determination to honour her long standing commitment turned out to be wrong. His assumption had been that his wife would very reluctantly arrange an alternate to manage the event.

He'd been sure she'd come because he had developed a habit of believing other people's work and priorities, compared to what he did, were not difficult or important. He had timed the trip so she would be torn. But he expected her to come.

This was after Reece had initially demurred on the trip deploying a range of cobbled together excuses ranging from her own part time work commitments, some social engagement she planned to urgently arrange that afternoon and the implausible allegation she wanted to do some preparatory reading for the looming start of her penultimate year in Highschool. She tossed that in because she knew that so far into her response he would have stopped listening.

His reaction was a familiar adventure into the kind of unpleasantness she had worked at becoming entirely inured to and had achieved being unemotional about. However he began to badger her, and she reverted to a rare, more aggressive alternative. She let him know what she thought of his idea and provided a few other choice observations which would, she hoped, kill it.

This wasn't a proposition he was going to let die however. Her response, and what she was wearing while she made it, gave him an idea that made him wonder why he hadn't arranged things that way in the first place. This led him to make an offer she couldn't refuse. Jake.

Now he was in the air. Without Tammy. After a brief uncertainty about what to do, he recalibrated his thinking and decided that she could be the one who would be left behind. That would work.

The plane, though a few years old was fast, had a long range and was fully tax deductible, though this did little to offset it's drain on the business. Even as they were taxiing to take off Reece started to feel sleepy. Unusual for her in mid-morning. As it was for Jake.

The rancher woke up a long time later. Awoken by Hansen rousing Reece.

He was trying to strike a balance between shaking her, speaking clearly enough to wake her, but avoid awakening Jake over the hum of the engine. Jake maintained the appearance of sleep because the first thing he noticed when he woke was that the plane was being buffeted by strong winds. Rain was pelting down on the windscreens and windows. All around them it was a solid dark grey. They were in a storm. And strangest of all, he'd been sleeping on a plane, which he never did.

Reece awoke, let out an epic yawn, looked around and said. 'Dad?' The question in her tone was about the situation the plane was in. She had flown on a few occasions with her him. Usually in the back, pretending to listen to music while he talked endlessly at clients or managers. It was revelatory and explained why the business had high turnover of personnel and he was constantly needing to find new clients. She'd never been in this kind of weather.

'Bad weather. But I get tired of flying around the storms Reece.'

'How long till we land.'

'A few minutes.'

Reece was relieved. She wasn't an expert on the relationship between light aircraft and weather, but she was certain this was well beyond what they were supposed to be flow in.

Hansen's voice had many tones. Few of them pleasant to listen to. This was new though. It was desolation. A business sliding into bankruptcy and the longest serving and most senior member of his management team had given him a scathing assessment of his capabilities as a businessman and character as a human being.

He was going to set up as a rival with every expectation that much of his current client base would follow and very likely some of his best employees. Hansen was forced to accept the longest serving employee and long-suffering General Manager was the main reason many had stuck with the business.

The collapse of his professional life put his personal life in stark relief. And so a future of bleakness was all he could foresee. And poverty or worse dependence on his wife which he feared most. For all the abundant evidence to the contrary, he believed this was not of his doing. He had a family, employees and clients that had conspired to bring him to this place. In part because of jealousy and in part he had been unfortunate to have his life populated by the unappreciative, disloyal and meanspirited.

So when he said. 'You never loved me.' To Reece it wasn't posed as a question. 'Never showed me any affection.'

Reece processed this for a minute. As with many things, facts inconvenient to Hansen's narratives didn't exist. As a child she had good memories of her him and mother. Separately and together. And she was careful to remember them so that her retreat from the family wasn't informed only by blame.

Rather preference based on what she observed in the present. Reece was unusual for her careful, almost meticulous examination of perspectives.

'We had some good times when I was little. Things have changed…yeah.'

'And why was that Theresa?'

She was annoyed as well as being a little anxious. The plane was being tossed around in the storm, and she imagined he had contrived the setting for this very conversation. There was lightning cracking in the sky around them. He had promised a family holiday only to position her as a captive audience for a heavy conversation like this. 'I think it was about the time I started to have a mind of my own Opinions. Points of view.'

'Things went south. Around when you and mom decided it would be a good relationship strategy to spend very little time together a as family. And when you two are together you're at each other's throats. Neither of you spend much time at home because you both work so hard. And no…I didn't ask you to do that, nor do I prefer we have nice things. Couple of reasons for you mixed in there maybe dad?'

These details were apparently inconsequential to the major failing he'd identified on her part. 'And now you don't love me anymore.' As if her observations were insubstantial and what she did was an intentional ploy to make his life miserable.

Now she was angry. Lightning hit the plane, and the rain was pelting on the machine, so she had to raise her voice as it bucked in the wind. Reece managed her life so that it was rare she could be in situations where people could corner her. But when they did, she was more than ready and never stepped back. 'I don't even like you. How you can be surprised by any of this is… a mystery to me. What are you a sleepwalker? What you should do dad is make a recording of how you speak to people. Any people. And listen to it and try to break through these delusions you have about yourself and imagine if you were on the receiving end of it.

You're an unpleasant person. That I can cope with. It's reasonably common. It's the fact that it's everyone else's fault that you don't like where you've landed in life. Arrogance and martyrdom are a bad combination it turns out dad.'

He turned to her nodding. 'Yeah. I had a…what do you call it. An epiphany I think it is. I'm…'

Even though he knew she was right he found it hard to say. 'I'm an unpleasant person.'

'Congratulation on the breakthrough dad. Can we get out of this fucking storm now.' Reece rarely used profanity around her parents as a part of her habit of given them nothing to find fault with. When she did, they knew she was putting a stake in the ground, and it wasn't going to move.

He continued as if she'd said nothing. 'But I didn't…I'm not the cause of you being…what you are. Things would have been different if you and your mother had been different. But you're both the same. You. Tammy. Unpleasant people. That's all we are Reece. And him.' He half turned his head towards the back. 'Always undermining me. Making me look bad.'

This was the same narrative she had heard for years but more overt. Even when he was willing to acknowledge he had some fault it only existed because of those surrounding him. He'd managed to fully and finally tear to shreds the good memories she had so assiduously preserved of him. 'Anyone makes you look bad dad. They don't try. People simply have to be alive and it happens. And if mom's a bitch around you that's between you and her.'

She had more. 'Unlike you I grew up and grew out of the self-centredness of childhood. I grew out of your games dad. You can't pin the shitty outcomes of your life on me because you know nothing about me. All you know about me is that I'm someone barely there.'

'And you're saying being that way isn't contrived to hurt me. And your mother.'

'It's contrived so that you don't infect me you fucker!' Reece had never been so angry. And so she failed to grasp the situation she was in.

'All that I did for you and your mother. For years. You only took it. And now I know what it was worth.'

'I didn't ask you to do anything. I didn't ask to be here. Everything you've done has been a vanity project about your ego.' Her analysis of her father all came tumbling out.

It had been refined over the yeas however she never thought she would lay it out for him. 'You work so hard because you do such a lousy job with people. You need to work three times harder to make the same dollar someone else makes who knows how to be pleasant. I'm counting the days. Marking them in a calendar. For the last three years, waiting for the day I can walk out of that dystopian mess you think is a home.'

He was quiet for a long term. 'Theresa. You won't need to worry about me, your mother or that calendar you've got anymore.' He pushed the yoke forward and the plane was immediately in a steep dive.

Jake had been continuing to appear to be asleep but listening intently. He didn't hear everything that Hansen said, but Reece had a voice that was sharp and clear. It could be cutting and sometimes insensitive to the wounds that it left. He wasn't so caught up in the dynamic, so he had begun to suspect where things were headed while Reece thought it was only an order of magnitude greater example of Hansen's habit of nasty entrapment.

Suspecting what he was going to do was one thing. Experiencing the plane go into an almost vertical dive and responding to it were quite another.

At least he was thrown forward against the narrow partition between the lounge and the cockpit. On which he cracked his head. Hansen was holding his arms straight pushing the yoke forward with his shoulders back so Jake could easily throw his arm around the man's neck. Pulling him back away from the controls was hard. Because they were diving steeply. Hansen let himself fall forward as soon as he felt the arm around his neck. This aided him in keeping the main control of the plane pushed down hard.

Jake worked outdoors every day. And he was used to working with stock in the pastures and the yards so he had good reflexes. He used his free hand to push against the partition which came halfway across the back of the pilot's seat and wrenched Hansen back hard away from the controls. At the same time calling out to Reece. 'Take the…wheel or whatever it's called and pull back.'

Hansen was thrashing around and instinctively let go of the control column and gripped the arm around his neck. He knew he was dealing with a man who was much stronger than he was and realised his only hope of being certain to realise his objective now rested with the foot pedals which he began to jab savagely. Reece had reacted quickly to Jake's call and was surprised that she was pulling hard on the yoke, yet the plane was responding only very slowly.

She had been allowed to take the controls of previous aircraft on a few occasions in the past and was surprised at how sensitive they were. Now the man in the pilot seat, in combination with the gale force winds was causing the plane to slide sickeningly sideways, buck and almost stall. Jake finally achieved his objective of pulling Hansen so far backwards and up out of his seat he couldn't reach any pedals. The plane continued to dive however they started to feel it shallow.

Suddenly the plane broke through the cloud cover, and they were headed for a landscape which, in their field of view, was simply white. This made it difficult to know how close they were to the surface. Finally, the plane started to respond strongly and the air, less turbulent at the lower altitude allowed it to level out and then climb. Once close to horizontal they could briefly see what kind of landscape they were in.

They started to climb, and they were aiming for the base of grey clouds, with occasional patch of blue now breaking them up. They were soon climbing more and more steeply. The Rancher was distracted by the fact that he had a decision to make. He made it. Hansen gave a few final jerks. Jake had done something he never thought he would. He had killed a man. Reece had the yoke pulled fully back.

She was also distracted by the death of Hansen but more so momentarily paralysed by fear and confusion. They were climbing steeply. Jake said, as calmly as he could manage. 'It's time to level off Reece.' He let go of Hansen and pushed her hand gentry forward. 'Level off now. Let's...take a moment.'

The plane slowly returned to simply being buffeted by a storm which was losing intensity.

Jake was about to extol her plane flying prowess when an alarm went off. Looking at the controls for the first time he noticed they were nearly all taped neatly over with black tape. He tried to reach forward but couldn't quite get to them. She saw what he was trying to do and ripped off the tape over the screen part of the console. The large rectangle of the radar screen came off with broken glass stuck to the tape. It had been smashed. Hansen wasn't taking any chances.

Under another piece of tape, the glass only cracked, the fuel gauge was in the red and the compass advised they were flying due north. 'I didn't think that looked like the outskirts of San Diego.' Said Jake. 'I suspect the radio is...'

She lifted the handset. The wire had been cut. 'Screwed.'

Jake nodded. This was either the end or the beginning of something. If it was a beginning he wanted to set the tone. 'You know one thing. this…individual…didn't factor in is we've got one of the finest pilots never to have flown an airplane.'

She had been about to demand that he take over. She picked up the tone of his voice. This was the moment to maintain control or fall to pieces. 'It would look good on my CV.'

'A nice sentiment Cowboy but you might recall I can't drive a car.' However he'd given her the impression he absolutely believed she could do it. Like Reece, he was someone who intentionally looked at various perspectives. It's why they had little respect for Hansen who only had one. And as part of that beginning, he wasn't going to take over as the leader. They were in this together.

'That would only confuse you. And all those video games I never played. Those and your natural talent.'

'Cowboy I've played Mario Brothers. And Minecraft. A bit of Fortnight I'll admit'

'I have no idea what any of those things are Reece, and yet I'm absolutely certain they're going to turn out to be one of the things that helps you get us on the ground…or whatever it was down there.'

He was telling her they were going to keep being the two people who had developed a natural affinity irrespective of age and geography. They would not revert to some stereotypes neither of them fit into. She nodded. They weren't going to take things too seriously either. She saw things become a challenge rather than an ordeal. 'I'm certain I can get us on the ground Cowboy.'

'It's the number of pieces you're in when I'm through with you that's a concern.'

'How hard can it be Reece.'

'Then why don't you do it.'

He laughed and put a little anxiety in his voice. 'Are you crazy. I'd never attempt to do something so dangerous. It's all on you. And you are going to do it with style.'

The grey they were flying through started to flash around them as they broke out of the clouds. They could see now they were flying over a huge lake, open water in most places, cracked off sheets of ice floating in others and a narrow solid sheet of ice on the western shore. In the distance was a range of mountains, quite a bit taller than the altitude they were at.

'Toto. I get a feeling we're not in Kansas anymore.' Said Reece.

Jake smiled. He realised however short a time they had left, he was going to get to know Reece like no one else had. 'Those mountains are way prettier than what I can see from the back porch on the ranch. But you know; I don't think we need a close-up view of them. Looks like our holiday turned into the adventure kind.'

'Maybe we turn south, burn as much fuel as we have at low altitude and then you can bring her down on one of the biggest landing strips on earth.'

Reece started with such a tentative turn on the yoke they barely changed course. She increased the turn very slowly and did some experimentation with the pedals so that soon they executed a gentle arc to take them south. What they saw was almost as daunting. Broken ice as far as the eye could see in front. But for the strip of solid ice on the shore. To the east land was a blur on the horizon.

'I packed for Sea World and Coronado Beach.'

Jake was wearing the heavy coat he'd left the Ranch in to take the long drive to join the trip he had been a little surprised to be invited on. Now that had been explained. 'And we'll still get there. Might take a little longer.'

The engine lost power briefly. 'First. We need to put this bird on the ground.'

'I'm assuming these pedals are a part of that process.'

'Although any ideas I have should not intrude on your piloting prowess, I think you've got plenty of runway. That sliding gearstick thing slows the engine down. It's all about taking things gradually.'

The plane stalled and surged again. 'Unless we fall out of the sky.'

'That might…accelerate the process.' They started to see they were in fact not so far from the end of the giant ice runway. 'Looks like the lake discharged into a river up ahead.'

'If in doubt, lose altitude.' She pushed the yoke forward and went into a dive. Not as steep as the one initiated by Hansen but steeper than intended. However, whether it had been her video game phase, a pastime she had been quite good at, or the natural aptitude Jake so convincingly argued she had, she stayed the course and pulled out to level off a few hundred feet from the ice. Then ignoring the more and more frequent surges, which were slowing airspeed further assisted by Jake reaching over and pushing the lever, she came down gradually. Watching the altimeter rather than the white plain she was landing on.

'Any final words Cowboy. Words of wisdom about planes would be handy around now.'

'I can say with absolute authority it's a good idea to keep them pointing straight rather than going…sort of sideways when you land them.'

'Roger that.' Reece's blood was getting loaded up with adrenaline.

She bounced heavily the first time. And they did feel the plane lurch sickeningly sideways. It bounced five more times. More and more gently then started to run smoothly on the ice. Jake slowly pushed the power lever all the way forward, they were still taxiing fast. Reece experimented with the foot pedals however the plane was not coming to a complete halt. She leaned over the dead body of Hansen slumped against the window, looked at the controls and hit a button which killed the engine.

The plane was slowing. Jake squeezed her shoulder, and she turned around and looked at him smiling. 'That was magnificent flying.' He said. As the last word was being spoken the plane dropped by about three feet below them.

'Shit.' Said Reece.

'We need to get out of here. Get the key so we can open the locker for the bags.' Jake realised Reece would have to come into intimate contact with Hansen's dead body. 'I can reach them. You go. We need to get as much weight out of the plane as possible.'

As she climbed over the seat she said. 'Bad time to decide you want to talk about my weight Cowboy.'

He looked at her. Mortified there had been such a misunderstanding. 'You're…shapely. In a good way.'

She laughed. 'That's exactly what I get called at school. Get those keys.'

When they were both outside, clear water was swirling around the plane. Jake was trying to open the cargo locker 'The wings should hold it up for quite a while but if the hatch goes under…' He was trying each of half a dozen keys.

He inserted a key and opened the hatch. That let in a flood of water however they were able recover the only three things in there. The bags they had brought and Reece's coat resting over the top of them. Hansen knew it would be a one-way trip and brought nothing. The hold often had camping, fishing and hunting gear. Not this time.

'I was hoping for more.' Said Jake. 'I should have got the first aid kit and cleared out the cooler with the food that was in there. The struts on the wings seem to be holding the plane up.' Reece pulled out the bags and Jake jumped aboard. There was six inches of freezing water in the cabin. He found the first aid kit.

The plane was stocked with a list of items for clients. There were chocolate bars, nuts and bags of chips which he put in the liner of the small bin for trash. He was thrown sideways as the starboard wing went down. The door he had climbed through was filling with water and he could immediately feel the plane being dragged down and crosswise. They were at the end of the long lake that discharged into a fast-flowing river under the ice, and it was pushing hard against the fuselage which pulled the wing down. He pushed roughly over Hansen's remains and opened the pilots door. He threw the first aid kit and bag of food out onto the ice and pulled himself onto the top of the plane as the cabin filled. However it was angling so he was balanced awkwardly on the top corner. If he rode it down it would slide him right into a pond of black swirling water. He saw the hole the plane had made in the ice was smaller at the tail section and he jumped towards it. He wrapped his arms around the top of the vane. He knew he had only one opportunity.

He stood on the tail wing and could see it was going under too quickly in the fast flow. He had to go as soon as he'd pulled both feet out of the water. He pushed off as hard and high as he could, but his feet slipped from under him.

His got far enough so his chest landed on the ice in a jarring landing and his head hit the rock-hard surface. However his waist was at the waterline and the current was relentless.

There was nothing to purchase on though he tried to claw at the ice. However enough of his body was in the river that it pulled him down, dragging him in. His hands were sliding, and he was slipping backwards. He expected to be looking up at the ice from below for the few minutes it would take him to die as he was dragged along under it. His shoulders were disappearing under the black water.

Then a hand came flying forward and grabbed his collar and pulled. The ice had cracked around the plane and the bags and Reece had nearly gone into the river, so she had hastily picked them both up and slide them away. She saw Jake jump to the to the tail section and she started to run the short distance around behind it because she knew he had seconds to jump. She jumped shortly after he did and threw out her hand for his collar, terrified for a moment her momentum would cause her to slide right into the river with him.

The landing hurt, but she held his head above water which now only had to flow around his neck. She was able to hold him while lying flat on her belly on the ice.

'There's a lighter in a little pocket on the left side of the pack. Try to get a fire started as quickly as you can. You can get out of here Reece. Keep going south girl.'

'We both get out of here or neither of us do Cowboy. Plus, you've got my knife in your pocket, and I want it. I'm going swing my other arm over and get two hands on your collar and then you bring both arms up together fast and grab my arms.'

He could feel himself slipping. His voice was filled with a sorrow that resonated even in that extremity. 'I'm going to die of hypothermia Reece.'

'You're going to try Cowboy. Now do it.'

He knew they would both go under soon so once she had both hands gripping his collar he kicked hard and swung his arms up together. His shoulders were out of the water which wasn't happy about it and was soon swirling all around him. 'Get hold of any of my clothes and pull yourself up.'

He reached forward in a huge push and took hold of her belt. The forces pushing him and pulling him were briefly balanced and he surged forward again with the other hand.

The first thing he could get any purchase on was a part of her body he would have preferred not to have taken hold of, but it served its purpose.

'We'll talk about the appropriateness of that later Cowboy.' She said this as she pulled her knees under herself, and he was able to get his hand around her thigh and pull his lower body onto the ice.

'Show me some skinny chick who could do that.'

Jake lay on his side and smiled. But the cold was like nothing he had ever felt. It was painful rather than numbing. He looked to the shore. It was quarter of a mile. 'Try to run. I'll bring your bag.'

He got up and started to stagger as fast as he could. How could it get even colder? He was sure it would prove too far. He fell over and felt himself being dragged along the ice, he got onto his hands and knees and she helped him up and he staggered forward a hundred yards and blacked out. He regained consciousness enough to feel rough spikey grasses in the back of his neck. 'Cowboy. Try to get up. We need to get close to something we can start a fire with.'

Jake's mind was deep in the fog, but he forced himself to get up.

He was drawn along a few dozen paces and started to fall. He felt Reece catch him as he lay down. He looked across at the vegetation at eye level. There was a plant low to the ground that had a canopy of leaves over very fine dead twigs which were perfect as to get a fire started. 'Get a pile of that stuff and light it up. But you'll need bigger dry twigs and branches gradually to get it going.' He was trembling uncontrollably and knew he was about to lose consciousness for the last time. 'Good luck Reece.' She wasn't there to hear it. She started running and based on what she saw, she would need to drag him a little further.

He was surprised to wake up at all. And to feel warm. Then he was even more surprised to find he was on fire. His Jacket was ablaze, and he could smell the unpleasant aroma of burning hair. What had woken him up though was being hit by a pine tree brow hastily torn from a tree. The pine needle covered branch was flailing away at his torso, except when less well aimed blows hit on the side of his face. Now that he was awake, he was able to roll over and over a few times on the low, cold, damp vegetation and the flame went out.

He looked around and could see he'd been dragged a few hundred yards from the shore.

He was only a few feet away from a dead tree that had fallen up against another tree and had enough dead wood piled under it to get it to catch fire. Creating heat from above as well as the fires around him. It eventually burned through and broke apart. It had been this that had caused him to catch alight.

Fortunately, Reece was returning, dragging a large branch from another dead tree behind her and stopped the flames from spreading. In addition to the dead tree, he saw half a dozen trees in a semicircle around him had caught fire. Under a few that had only started to burn he could see that they'd had piles of dead wood placed at the base. There was no wind, and it had rained the day before, so the fire didn't spread. But with a strong source of flames at the base and the oils in the tree with a bit of effort they could be brought to burn individually.

He looked up to see a sixteen-year-old covered in grime and soot, breathing heavily and smiling. 'Sorry about the hair…and the beard.'

'I wanted to try out short hair anyway.' He stood up and gave her a hug. Their first 'And it is nice to be alive.'

He laughed. 'And warm.' At that moment he heard a sound and looked at one of the trees which had been burning a long time.

He had spent most of his life on the land, some of it fighting or lighting fires. He clasped Reece by the hand and ran. One of the larger trees on fire broke off at its trunk which had been partially rotten and, spinning around as it fell, landed where they'd been standing. It hit the ground and sent up a huge shower of sparks.

They started to laugh. 'You picked a good time to wake up.' Reece sat on the ground. She was exhausted. Jake sat down, and leaned his back on hers and sat quietly for quite a while.

He said. 'I think this is the kind of campfire we need every night. We might have to wake up and keep up with it now and again. I like the idea of lighting up the trees.'

'I read it in a book called Kirby. She was tough. It'll beat the hell out sitting in the dark dressed for southern California. I expect you to go and skin a mountain lion or a wolf or a bear or something. It can wait till morning though.'

'Some people are afraid of dentists. I find bears a bit scarier myself.'

'I'll handle the bears then. Never met a bear I didn't like.' She replied. Then yawned and added 'Never met a bear.'

Jake looked up at the stars for quite a while, as he enjoyed doing every night. He heard her breathing find the rhythm of sleep. He had no idea how long he'd been unconscious. It was nice having her lean against him. He was wide awake now and when he saw dawn starting to break an hour later he realised she'd been up through the afternoon and most of the night trying to get him warm, eventually on an industrial scale. Once he could see enough to move around, he gently settled her onto the ground and made a pillow of his jacket, though he was immediately very cold. He hoped his bag hadn't gone under some burning trees. He found it near the lake shore. He also hoped hers had not succumbed to the ice that opened around the plane. But it was there, as was the first aid kit and food. He recovered it all. He was pleased about the first aid kit and chocolate, but unsure it had been a sensible thing to do given it had led to the risk of Reece facing the situation alone.

She was awake standing near a place where two trees had crossed over where they fell where the fire was still burning brightly. 'We'll need to conserve what we have. However. Should we start this…ah…adventure with half a candy bar each.'

'You read my mind. I was worried you were going to suggest we cut it into twenty pieces.'

'That was going to be my suggestion for the other ones.'

'Starvation by candy bar. There are worse things that could happen. Like a bear who decides to become a dentist.' They stood by the fire, enjoying what they suspected was going to be their biggest meal for quite a while. 'How far do you think it is to…anywhere.'

'Well.' Said Jake. In the slightly exaggerated way an experienced older man might. 'Based on the cruising speed of that plane, the direction it was travelling, the number of hours we were asleep maybe an allowance for a head wind in the storm.' He took off his hat and scratched his head theatrically. 'I can be confident in saying…I have no idea where we are.'

'Thanks for not trying to reassure me Cowboy.'

'In less…unusual circumstances I'd say we'd wait near the plane. However, I suspect Russell will have disabled the transponder. Hence. I think the only plan my poor old head can devise is we walk south.'

'For…?'

He shrugged and smiled. 'Month or so maybe. Two at most…also maybe.'

'Easy. What could go wrong?'

'Blizzards, big rivers we can't cross, bears, wolves, my lighter runs out of gas…'

She broke in. 'It was rhetorical Cowboy.'

'Yeah. And there's whole food thing.'

'Yep. Looks like it's me and you against the world.'

'If I was the world I'd look out.'

'We're going to kick its ass.'

Seven days later they had run themselves out of candy bars, nuts and chips no matter how small they tried to make the pieces. They'd talk occasionally but both had crafted a lifestyle in which talking to someone wasn't central to having a good day.

'I watched a program once that said fasting was good for you. It wakes up your brain because it's not natural to have food available all the time.' Jake said.

'My brains loving this. It's wide awake and shouting in my ear. Get me some food you dumb bitch.'

'I'm getting similar feedback.'

'I'm missing my 'shapely in a good way' body. Partly because my clothes don't fit now and it's draughty and I've realised skinny people don't have any fuel in the tank for a long walk in the woods.'

'Skinny people are dumb.'

'I find them annoying.' They saw a dear in the distance through a lightly wooded area beside the river they were walking beside. They both stopped. 'Meeeeeeeeeaaaaaat.' Reece whispered this every time they saw one.

Cowboy decided to introduce something, as an interesting fact rather than an idea. And see how she responded. 'Back in the caveman days, so I believe, the people couldn't outrun game, but they used their numbers and they'd outsmart it. They would have people stationed along the way and use some natural barrier to work against then scare the game into the area. One caveman, or cavewoman would run them until they were exhausted with more cavepeople ready to take up the chase, maybe some more less good at running along the way to stop it veering off. On and on with the whole tribe involved. Then they'd be able to kill it when it was exhausted. Or run it over a cliff.'

Reece nodded thoughtfully. 'Interesting.' She felt her back pockets. 'Damn. I left my tribe of cave people in my other pants.' They laughed. Then she said. 'You tell me where to run. I am willing to try anything. My brain is trying to convince me we are as smart as a tribe of cave people which I think is probably not showing them the respect they deserve. Especially when it comes to chasing deer around.'

Jake squinted when he thought. 'Okay. We use the river as the barrier. One of us jogs out wide first and a good way south. Then the other one runs up behind her and keeps up as best they can and far enough out from the river to try to stop her turning away from it. The person behind is making a hell of a racket. The one in front hears them, spots the deer and takes over. The first runner rests while the other one tries to turn the deer towards the river and then back to the north down to the first runner who tries to do the same thing. Hopefully it'll be slowing down a little. All along we're calling out and we never lose touch with the sound of each other's voices. We keep doing that until she either dies of exhaustion or...'

'We do.'

'Exactly.'

'Sounds easy.' Reece nodded earnestly. 'Could you run that by me again after the part where we use the river as a barrier.'

'Of course. I may not describe it in the same way the second time because I found it confusing.'

After they'd gone through it again Reece added. 'We call left and right based on her left and right.'

'An important detail.' They looked up. The deer was gone.

'Damn.'

'Reece that piece of meat belongs in our bellies. Come up slowly and I'll go out wide. Whichever one of us sees it we start the caveman shuffle.'

They both walked forward. Jake was five hundred yards from the river and a long way forward when Reece came across the animal which bolted to the open forest. 'She's breaking loose.' Reece ran in a wide arc southeast away from the deer. She saw the animal as it slowed and yelled loud enough for it to be frightened and turn and she ran as fast as she could behind it. Jake had run wide and came in with enough speed for the animal to see him on her left and turn straight towards the river. He kept running forward as fast as he could.

She had disappeared but he kept running for five minutes and caught up and saw she was slowing about a hundred yards from the shore. He ran wide and forward and then came back towards her on a tangent and tried to turn her north. She turned east but came up against a small lake which was an overflow of the river when the spring thaw swelled the flow and the deer found herself pushed back towards it. He skirted the lake and continued wide so he could barely see her. 'She's coming back down. A hundred yards off the river.' He didn't know where Reece was, but he was spent.

Reece was out as wide as she thought she should be. She saw the deer but wouldn't be able to get in front. She tried to follow it and ran in at an angle to push her back towards the river. Reece had never run so fast in her life. There were no trophies and ribbons in her room but not because she couldn't have won any if she'd put her mind to it. Now she was getting a huge rush of both excitement and an implacable desire to survive she had never experienced. As the deer pulled out of sight, she ran wider in the hope of intercepting it if it turned. But she'd lost sight of it. The timber was denser. She realised she and Cowboy needed to be careful or they would lose each other. She kept running in between interludes of walking. And calling.

Reece heard him coming in the distance behind her, so she continued forward more slowly. And then there it was.

The deer had stopped in a thicket and was huffing in a way not so different to her. Reece immediately moved away so she could get around north of the deer and come in pointing half south and half towards the river. She picked up a branch and came in screaming and calling out to Jake what she was doing. The deer leapt forward, trying to break north but getting such a fright Reece turned it south. At a shout it lost its footing and slid sideways, landing on its side heavily but was up in seconds and running.

Reece was spent and she was losing sight of the deer but she heard. 'I see her.' Jake had been walking down towards the action but slowly and recovering his breath just in case. He was far enough out to keep abreast and drive her closer to the water. There was a log the deer jumped with ease. There was a slippery stone Jake fell over. He got up and ran, but she was gone, and he hadn't seen in what direction. They were both too tired to try to find it.

'Come up to me.' He waited while Reece came. 'I lost her. We gave it a good run though.'

'She would have been tough anyhow.'

'I find venison a little gamey myself.'

'What does gamey taste like.'

'I'll cook up a rooster for you when we get back.' They were walking towards their bags when they heard a huffing sound.

'I can do gamey.'

'It has its charms.'

Without a word they spread out and walked forward. The animal was flagging as much as they were but was a long way from beaten. It turned and leapt away but sharing a glance the two hunters spread out further and started calling. After five minutes Reece called out. The deer has run up against a small ridge. It might have climbed it, but Jake was suddenly there shouting so she ran along the ridge which pushed its way out into the river. Reece cut off any retreat north of the ridge, so the deer ran out onto the riverbank. Her hooves and body weren't made to run on the round stones along the river which had collected up in front of what was a rugged cliff face below some stunted pines projecting into the angry waters. She'd gone far enough out to be cornered by the two bipeds. All three stopped, breathed deeply and considered their options.

'What now.'

'It's not going to be pretty. But now we take a lesson from the Hyena. We take turns running in at her to make her try to climb that ridge which she'll never do. The other holds back. She'll be slow trying to get around us on the river stones. One of us should hold her I hope.'

It wasn't pretty. They took turns running and shouting at a terrified and exhausted animal. It did make pathetic attempts to climb up the rocky cliff a mountain goat could have scaled easily. Finally she fell back from trying to leap up the shortest section of the cliff and amazingly nearly succeeded in her last desperate bid for freedom. She tried to turn and land on her hooves but landed awkwardly with a foreleg caught between boulders. The bone snapped which brought her down. Seeing her laying on her side unable to get up with three legs flailing and the terrified calls she made was the most heart wrenching thing Reece had ever witnessed.

'This is when she's at her most dangerous Reece.' Cowboy was not being patronising. Reece could see it would be easy to get in the firing line of one of those hooves. He picked up a rock twice the size of a baseball and approached from the head. He struck the animal at base of the skull at the meeting point with the neck several times hard. It happened very quickly, and the animal was still.

Reece came over and was surprised to see the older man's eyes wet with tears. 'It's my least favourite thing on the farm. There I have a gun and I have enough time to…' He shrugged. '…it's a silly little thing, but I thank them for the meat.'

Reece knelt beside him awkwardly on the stones. She'd seen a deer once in petting zoo. This was bigger and it was a beautiful animal. She stoked it's sides. 'Thanks for your meat.'

Cowboy covered it's eyes. Reece though it might be because he didn't want her to look at the animals head, which was not as bad as she'd though it might be. But he said. 'What you call a deer with no eyes.'

She hadn't been expecting this and shrugged. 'What.'

'No I-deer.'

'Oh Jesus.'

He cut the animals throat and started to bleed it for a while. Then he cut down the belly and gutted her and cleaned out the cavity.'

'Not being as conversant as you with butchering and eating what was running around free and happy a little while before, what's the plan.' Said Reece.

'My I-deer is…'

'No. No. That was a one-time thing only.'

'Ah. My approach is that we should protect this meat, stop walking and live off it until it's runs out, except what we're able to dry. We can't carry it fresh in these temperatures without it spoiling and I think we need to rest and build up condition or we're…'

'Screwed.'

'Pretty much. My…idea…is that somewhat counter intuitively we climb part the way up that mountain to get near the snowline but still in the trees and bring down enough snow to keep this girl chilled down and stop her sending out a message for some of the neighbours to come and help themselves.'

Reece looked up. 'Two hours with half a deer each.'

'A good estimate. I can probably carry the deer over my shoulders which is easier than if she's cut up. How do you think you'll go with the bags.'

'Roast meat at the end of the climb. Sure. The idea of having some time off walking is a great I-deer. We get one each at that.'

The animal was large and heavy, and it took four hours, and the long dusk, though shortening, helped them make it with enough light and time to collect some wood. By the time they had found a camp and brought down enough backpacks of snow to cover her inside a hollow in the rocky soil it was fully dark. Reece managed the fire as she turned out to be very good at it. She would pick up the most suitable material all through the day. Towards the end they would gather enough wood to get things started. Her aim was to flick down the flint on the lighter, have what she'd set lit for the count of one, and be ready to go through a process of gradually building it up. They'd light a fire for themselves first and then some trees in a ring if it wasn't windy. They weren't concerned about starting a forest fire because if there was a chance someone might notice that it would be fine with them. However they didn't want to start one and get caught in it. Jake had made a bed of snow, and he started skinning the animal. He could have cut it up first, but he wanted the skin whole. So Reece brought down more snow while he did this. And then; heaven.

'How do you like your steak.'

'Sooner rather than later so I guess that means rare.'

'Pink in the middle.' The were toasting strips of venison on the fire. 'I plan to eat as much as my body will let me, get this fire roaring and go to sleep until I'm cold and repeat the process.'

'We have exactly the same plan.'

The deer lasted five days. Jake scraped as much of the fat and flesh from the skin and, lacking the salt the other solutions to cure it the way he usually did, he used some gritty dirt and melted snow to rub and then wash it from the slush puddle left when they relocated the meat. They cut some fine strips of meat to dry which was very slow in the cold air, so they made a rack over the fire that sat high enough above the coals and made it smoky to help the meat slowly cure. They'd found a topic of conversation which was engrossing. Running down and killing animals. They talked about what was learned from the No I Deer. What they might do better What could they do without a river

They talked through the short list of animals they knew of that might be encountered. Though northern Canada had many more they'd not heard of.

'What about a moose.'

'We run away.'

'Pack of Wolves.

'We think about how much fun we've had on this trip and say goodbye.'

'Bear?'

'Pray.'

'Not much besides deer really.'

'I think we could find a way to catch some fish. Or ducks maybe. These rivers are too fast but if we come upon a tributary or the lakes we're starting to see it might be worth trying things if we're resting and eating dried deer for a while.'

'I never thought I'd say it, but I could use a break from venison. It's a bit gamey.'

'You'll know what gamey is if we ever caught an old buck. But they'd have a bit more endurance I'd say.'

After four days rest and with another four of dried meat in their packs they struck out again. The first objective was to find a place to have a wash once the sun had at least some warmth. Soon they were clean and dressed and ready to walk. The deer hide had not fared well, but Jake kept trying to get make it useable. They decided to take turns with it which was cut as a simple long coat.

Two armholes and a few strategic slits with sinews to tie it shut. It was surprisingly warm but; 'Didn't smell great.' They weren't sure if taking their turn was a good thing or not. However it did start to get more supple with wear and either it started to smell less or they started to smell more. They acclimatized.

It was decided to make their best attempt and being cave people hunters.

'I heard an old Indian saying once. White man walks much and sees little. Red man walks little and sees much.

'To paraphrase that. We should slow down?'

'Less elegant but I think so.'

'Not like we're in any hurry to get anywhere. School's gone back in, so I've got months in front of me.'

'Yeah. It's the thing that comes after Autumn that might be a problem.'

After half an hour Cowboy was directed to look in a specific location. 'What's that.' Reece said.

'I think it's called a marmot.'

'Let's try and kill it and eat it.'

The Marmot got away but the next day they found some eggs and Jake, though reluctant to blunt the knife, started to whittle some straight sticks he found into spears. A day later they ran down and stuck a badger. 'I don't think you need to cook me a rooster.' Said Reece.

They stopped at each lake, of which there were far too many, as they needed to decide how to navigate around them. And where to skip stones. One each, at each lake. Reece's ability to skip stones, once she had some practice was, Jake advised; spooky. 'I've skipped stones with a lot of people, and I don't usually need to try to count that fast.'

'I'm set for life. There's big money is skipping stones I believe.'

'I find money to be overrated. Until I run out of it. Then I learn important it is.'

'I may have to have stick with being a pilot. Take Offs: Zero. Flights: One. Landing in which plane survived: Zero.'

'I didn't like the colour scheme of the interior of that plane. The leather seats clashed with the carpet.'

'The booze was crap.'

'Stones.'

'Say what?'

'Stones. We should be throwing them. When you said 'crap' it reminded me of a novel I read once. I didn't finish it. Terrible editing. But I got up to the part where these Ogres, which in this case were a very pleasant, hunted by throwing stones at things. They got so good they could break an Elf's leg at twenty yards.'

'I like that. Never warmed to elves. What's the word…supercilious.'

'That is my new go to word for elves. Funnily enough that's exactly how they were in the book.'

'Let's start killing things with rocks.'

They were initially driven by hunger, however they slowly got better at first hearing, then seeing, then understanding the tracks and traces of more and more wildlife. They had one spear each and several short sticks carved to a point and always carried the best rock they could find in their hand. Two were never needed because there wasn't a second chance. Over the weeks that followed they ran away from a moose and ran towards some coyotes who came to visit their camp.

They were getting enough to eat so they chased some elk for fun. They had no hope of catching one. Though they did strategise for hours about it.

It turned out that the defences of the porcupine worked well for most animals, but not their sharp sticks. They would cook the animal whole and carefully pull away the meat. Which was delicious.

They'd been walking for seven weeks. They practiced throwing their sharp spears, which they made heavier versions of. If they injured something they would finish the animals off stabbing with the short ones, of which they carried two or three in their belts. Partly to do anything to save the knife which was getting narrower. They had stone throwing competitions, eventually able to wound some ducks enough to catch them. They tried to spear and throw stones at Canadian geese, catch river otters before they went into their dams and dig out a variety of burrowing animals.

It was getting cold. The snow line on the mountains around them was lowering. They came to the bank of a river they were walking towards and saw something through the bushes. 'There is one great thing about Canadian rivers in Autumn.' They walked a bit further and could see what they'd both seen on many a documentary. A river with rapids, boulders and short waterfalls with salmon leaping up against the flow.

'I'm going to see if I can catch one.' Said Cowboy. Reece had thought he would do this by trying to spear one of the throng of fish in some of the pools waiting their turn to leap forward. But he wanted to see if he could have one jump right into his backpack. It took him half an hour. They were both laughing as he moved the bag round barely to miss one, have another go in the bag and flap out and one leap up and hit him in the chest nearly knocking him off the rock. Finally a large fish wagging in the air went into the bag and was shut tight behind it. They had eaten that morning, but that fish was cooked and eaten within half an hour.

'Tired of walking.'

'I'm surprised how much I've grown to like it. However. I could use a break that's for sure.'

'How about we ice down a bunch of fish and smoke them so we've got a full pack of food and get going in a week or so. This salmon is full of fat and protein. It's getting colder but we need to rest and put on some condition. We could follow these rivers, but they may not lead to habitation. They seem to head west.'

'South is simple and we need a break.'

Because of the way they lived, when food was plentiful they had learned to eat well beyond the satisfaction of hunger.

They would eat and eat and had decided if there was only one thing to eat they would look for something else while they were eating it.

They were not the only ones enjoying the largesse of the salmon, many were dying and washing up on the riverbank. After a spectacular rock throw by Jake they tried River Otter but it combined oily with gamey and they were cute so they stuck with the fish. They gathered during the day and dried the meat through the night. Now accustomed to the howls of the wolves which had meant they needed to take turns sleeping. There was always drying and smoking meat to attend to.

After five days they were confident they had as much dried food as they could carry, and they were in the best condition they could expect to be. Both noticing how quickly it was possible to gain weight when one was eating most of the waking hours. Returning to their camp after washing was a sight they had dreaded. A bear was pawing the rocks they covered their stores of dried fish with and eating large quantities of it.

Deciding that running up to a bear and yelling at it wasn't a good plan, they moved away and made a fire and looked into it for a while. 'How high can those animals climb.' Said Reece eventually.

'Depends on their weight I guess.'

'We're not going to let a bear beat us.'

'Nope. Even though we have gained a few pounds you'd be able to get higher than a bear. The cold is coming after us from the north. But I think maybe we spend another three days. Lift the work rate since we're rested and well fed. Get those packs full and go.'

'That bear is not shapely in a good way.'

'Pear shaped.' Said Jake.

They were both quietly pleased that when something went wrong, in this case seriously wrong, one or both didn't treat it like a disaster that would diminish their chances of survival even if it did. Survival was hard enough without adding frustration and anxiety to it. 'It's weird.' Reece said. 'I miss walking. I thought I'd never want to walk again but we see so much and it's so beautiful and quiet and every day I get to try to get up close to very beautiful animals, kill them and eat them. It's like I found my true calling.'

'I'm having much the same experience. If we weren't lost and experiencing the fear of dying at any moment from a variety of causes, this would be my idea of fun.' Replied Jake.

'We can thank that asshole who's now a popsicle in his plane for something.' She had not mentioned Hansen. Jake had thought she might be sensitive, even considering his malign intentions. And the rancher had killed him right in front of her. However by the sound of her voice, she'd move on. And it hadn't been very far to go.

They returned to the camp to find everything in disarray and their backpack shredded. Jake felt foolish for not anticipating this. At least he always carried the knife, and Reece always carried the lighter which were their two most precious possessions. Jake had already made one sling bag for carrying food, so now he would make another from their rest of the deer. They chased a coyote away and Reece said. 'If bear slobber won't kill us I'd say we could salvage a couple of days' worth out of this.'

'Great. Let's pack it up, move camp and find a tree that's not going to support this one or any of his friends to climb.'

'Hey. Look at this. He was a technophobe bear. The phones are okay. The screen of mine is a bit more cracked than it was. Shame we can't charge them. The thing I miss most from the modern world is listening to some tunes.'

Once they'd decided to do something there was no uncertainty. They got it done together. They had to spend time to pick a camp they could defend and made several piles of wood in a circle and some up against some trees. When the wolves got too curious, they would light the whole area up and pick up the spears they had for throwing. The heavier sticks, almost like pikes, were for defence if the wolves or some other predator came close. There was fierce competition to spear a wolf for the pelt. But the wolves were wily. And at that time mainly curious. There was a bounty of fish and the animals that come to the shores to feed on them. However the hungry times of winter were approaching. And they may not be cowed by sharp sticks then.

They worked hard all day. Catching the fish was work, but it was also a lot of fun to be catching so many fish. After that first night, they had adopted a curious approach to sleeping. They made a layer out the softest grass or leaves they could find to sit on and then slept back to back. One was always awake.

When they got sleepy, they woke the other. That went on all night, even if they could only do an hour each that's the way it had to be. It was usually wolves or coyotes but sometimes a curious animal they would like to turn into a piece of meat arrived and if it was speared or run down in the moonlight it would be a cause, as always when they had success hunting, for celebration.

The bags were filled and they headed south and came across no more rivers or tributaries large enough for the salmon to run up. However they entered a world with thousands of lakes. They would talk for hours and strategize about some animals they would love to catch as their skill increased. They knew they would never get a moose. But a caribou, they thought they could do if they caught some in the right circumstances. It was almost becoming contrary to their main objective of walking back to civilisation as they'd have to stop and eat it and dry it if they did catch one. And eating a caribou would take a while. They decided that if they left some to the scavengers that would perpetuate the cycle of life enough to make it a fair outcome.

In open country they could only hope to run a herd or small group into rough terrain and try to get around them often enough and tire them out so that one might fall or an old or very young animal would become exhausted. They carried their heavy spears and would take their best shot. They knew enough to avoid the males in rut with their groups. But the herds tended to run rather than attack. They were an animal that could do forty miles an hour for a while which would leave the pair in the dust, unless they had a natural barrier on two sides and they could get a long way from each other to try to turn them back and forward within the barriers.

They had tried this three times and found it exhilarating but they were a long way from making a kill. They agreed it would be a good return on investment in terms of energy expended and when they were running about, they sometimes found birds eggs or even some lemmings and a badger on one occasion.

Early on they had realised that a diet of pure meat was not going to give them some of the nutrients they needed. However, neither of them was well versed in what was safe and what was not in terms of the various berries, tough fruits and tubers they found in swamps and saw the evidence of animals having dug up. So they decided to try to see what at least a few different animals had eaten and start eating small quantities themselves. Sometimes they learned this when an animal was interrupted browsing, however usually they examined what was in the guts of animals they'd killed

Soon they had broken nails from digging skinny tubers and pulling out some marsh plants once they were satisfied they were safe.

And a few greens they saw enough birds and small mammals eating to decide they would get their greens from the same sources. They knew as autumn deepened; these sources would be harder to find.

One day, walking though the open tundra they saw a heard of fifty or so Caribou in what they believed to be the best position they would get. Reece had become an expert at climbing trees high enough for no bear to be able to scale and they were in an area where bears were scarce because there was little prey for them. The herd was grazing so they had time to get what they had secure and sit down and make a plan. They didn't have a large stock of food left and they both knew they were going to spend a great deal of energy on a low probability undertaking. Yet it was what made their lives exciting and punctuated days of endless wilderness.

They went in different directions. Reece was going to get behind them and turn them away from the lake towards some broken country.

There was a line of rocky ground which a caribou might carefully walk over, but a running heard was not going to chance. However there was a gap covered in turf that would be a natural place to escape. Reece got them running as fast as she could between the lake and the rough ground and even though there was no way she could catch them she swung around behind them enough to cause them to naturally make for the gently sloping grassy plain through the gap. Once she knew they were committed she turned and ran back south as fast as she could. They were bunching up a little approaching the bottom of the pass when Jake appeared running down from the top and screaming and waving his pike with a shirt tied to it. He had to do it soon enough so they weren't so committed they would charge over him.

They pulled up into an untidy jostling of large animals confronted by a man screaming, shouting and zig zagging towards them swinging a flag. He wanted the herd to turn north along the lake because there were miles of broken hills to the east of the lake and once in what was effectively a corridor they hoped to be able to stay at either end of the herd, chasing them forward and back. Jake backed off during the confusion as they settled so they wouldn't decide to run either side of him.

But kept yelling and flying the flag. They broke south instead of North. If Reece was too close, they would simply run around or over her. She had sped away and looked back. Seeing them come towards her she kept running until they slowed and eventually stopped.

She stopped. And like them, rested for a while and then she ran at them again. She had a flag of skin on her pike and also ran in zig zags. But not fast. She wanted them to see her and have time to decide to move in the other direction. They did this and she stayed back as long as they were moving. This time Jake was nearly down on the plain at the mouth of the pass. All he wanted them to do was keep running straight instead of turn toward him. It was an easy decision for the animals in the lead. They were fast, but he was fresh and only needed to keep in sight of them from behind and keep them moving. Reece walked along slowly to make sure she was well past the grassy pass. Jake could not keep up but he was not far behind when they stopped and were all huffing dense steam into the air. He climbed up a place in the broken ground he could get over and travel north until he was able to come down half a mile above them. He was breathing heavily but he didn't want them to get much rest, so he charged down at them and they were soon in a panic and turning to run south.

It was difficult to judge distances, and the idea was to run them and let them settle for only a short time and then turn them and send them back. However the distance between Jake and Reece wasn't far enough so she had a herd of caribou charging at her and they hadn't had time to absorb the new threat that had appeared in their escape route. It was at that moment she realised how big these animals were, some with massive antlers, a few bright red which meant they were moulting. She slowed down and screamed and waved her flag. Caribou can swim well and fortunately for Reece the leaders decided to wheel west towards the lake. She recovered her senses and decided this was the only chance she was going to get. The animals slowed as those in front hit the water. Briefly she had a wall of jostling caribou in front of her. She ran in and without much time to choose drove her pike into the neck of an animal a dozen yards from the water. The heavy straight stick was torn from her hands while the caribou swung it's head from side to side so that it nearly came back around and smashed her in the face. The tail end of the herd was entering the water and pushed the injured animal along, so it was up to its knees the water even with her trying to get in front and turn it.

There was simply too much adrenaline in her system, and she ran in with one of the short dagger sticks they had and drove it also into the animals neck. Being so close she realised that this was a completely different proposition to the deer they had run down. The caribou had been mortally wounded by the pike but could swim far enough out to drown. It stopped now. Calling.

They stood looking at each other; both breathing heavily. Up close it was one of the most beautiful animals she'd ever seen. She was looking into it's jet-black eyes. She was gripped with an absolute need to be certain this animal didn't go to waste because of what she'd done. She needed to make certain it died as painlessly as possible and that she ate as much of it as she possibly could. She pulled another dagger stick from her belt and ran around behind, intending to drive it into its neck from the other side. But the Caribou spun around. Keeping watch and intent on defending itself. It felt a little silly because she kept running around, even knee deep in water, while it turned as she tried to get to the other side. She cut in close to achieve her aim and didn't keep far enough away so she was in range of a hind leg. It kicked sideways more than she expected, and a hoof crunched into her thigh and sent her sprawling. Fortunately it didn't hit her with the full force of a backwards kick. She was falling back when she saw Jake running in and full speed and adjusting his aim. Driving his pike, flag still fluttering, behind the animals ear.

It's front legs buckled. It's mouth near the shallow water huffing slowly. Blood pouring from its neck.

Running in he hadn't expected her to come around to the other side to try to stab the animal again. He saw her flying backwards as he adjusted his aim to behind the ear. He let go of the pike and turned, picked her up and moved away.

'Reece are you alright.'

She was in a great deal of pain however in the world they lived in now that was secondary. 'I'm fine. Except for being stupid.' She was getting angry with herself. 'I don't know if it broke my leg but I'm not going anywhere for a while. God damn it. Why did I have to do that.'

Jake was pressing into her leg firmly enough to be extremely painful, but she knew why. 'Don't think it's broken.'

'Bad enough so I'll be a liability.'

He smiled. 'That's the last time we need to hear about anything like that. That's not what this day's going to be remembered for Reece. This is the day you took on a fully grown Caribou with a stick and won the fight. It's a fight for survival. Getting hurt is part of that. The skin on that animal. It's going to wrap right around the both of us at night and its meat will keep us alive for a few weeks.

'One way to get a rest from walking I suppose.'

'I was growing weary of it.' The beast made a few heart-rending noises and fell sideways. It's chest was rising and falling, though only shallow now and not in the great heaves of a few moments before.

'Could you help me.' He knew why. He knew it was going to hurt and might even be a bad idea, but he held onto her while she hobbled next to the head of the beast. She was crying as she caressed the animals neck. 'Thank you for saving us.'

He took out his knife and glanced at her briefly in case she wanted to do it. She nodded. She took the knife, having watched Jake do it many a time. 'Hey Cowboy. What do you call a Caribou with its throat cut.'

He could not guess that one.

'A dead Caribou of course.'

They always managed a laugh, even a lame one, whenever the option was for things to get serious. 'Okay. You're going to skin…'

'Boo Boo. That's his name. Or at least that's what he'll be when he's a blanket.'

'You're going to skin Boo Boo while I do some running.'

'I'll bring our things down here and start collecting some of this driftwood and bring some in from the tree line. We'll be camping here tonight which means it could get interesting because we're going to have visitors who'd like a piece of Boo Boo.'

'We can get by without sleep because in addition to fending off a wolf pack we'll be drying meat all night and we'll take turns while we keep drying it and sleep through the day. Three days we'll be twenty pounds heavier and have as much as we can carry.'

Jake had taught her how to skin an animal and she found it was harder than it looked. He explained it was much harder with a blunt knife. He'd found a stone which, with hours of rubbing it together with a harder stone had created a very flat surface. It was nothing like his sharpening gear on the ranch, but it kept the knife functional.

'I'll gut Boo Boo here and try to drag him to where those bigger rocks are where you can sit. Hopefully the wolves will fill up on entrails tonight. Or it might attract more wolves.'

'Bring it on. Reece and Cowboy.'

'Against the world.'

Even gutted it was a heavy animal. They came to silent agreements about things. Reece would not bemoan the fact that she couldn't help because she was so stupid as to get injured. It achieved nothing. They would turn their attention to the tasks necessary for survival and if there was time try to make the other person laugh. When it was time to move, Jake didn't offer a stick or a shoulder for her to lean on. That would be inefficient. He came back, scooped her up and sat her on the rock which he had positioned Boo Boo near so she could reach out and very slowly and carefully cut the skin from the flesh. Trying to minimise the fat and meat left on it. This skin she would be making absolutely sure she didn't cut through. Which, given how blunt the knife was and the nature of the beast, she would be hard pressed to do. This hide was special.

When Jake said he would be running, he meant it. He had to protect what they already had and give them some chance of surviving the night with limited firewood, some of which would be needed to fend off wolves who wanted to take what they'd acquired. These things were concerning. They made him anxious to a degree. And yet he'd never felt so alive. He was fighting for his life with another person fighting just as hard.

The journey was much farther than he'd hoped and they'd done so much better than he'd believed they could. If they had to abandon Boo Boo and leave him to the wolves, they would still live to fight another day. However, he was going to throw everything he had at taking whatever they could. Partly because it was such a beautiful animal to kill for nothing and because he wanted Reece's courage to be vindicated.

He arrived back. They ate as much of their stores as they wanted. They wouldn't start a fire to cook Boo Boo until it was getting dark. Jake repositioned the carcass so Reece could keep going. She had time so they were going to take the skin all the way down the legs, all the belly and white neck and dewlap and right up to the antlers. Jake was bringing armloads of wood. Some a bit damp but they knew how damp it could be to dry by the fire and be able to throw it on late in the evening or early morning.

Some coyotes had found the guts and Jake was too busy to chase the away which was a shame. They weren't afraid of coyotes at least not yet. But Jake wasn't going to expend the energy scaring them off. The wolves would be different, so he kept bringing wood in, even when it started to look like they had a lot.

Boo Boo had been skinned and looked strange being an intact caribou with no skin. His face and antlers were fine.

Reece started to cut the meat into the strips they tried to make as thin as possible a few inches wide so it would dry quickly while they didn't have too many pieces to manage. They'd learned it was more efficient to spend time on the knife and cut thinner strips which would dry faster. The blade was only half as wide as it had been more than two months before.

She was making a pile of these strips of meat on a skin and another one of the yellow fat which they knew they should eat some of but couldn't face. Every trip Jake would stop. Have a little water and eat some of the surprising array of food they had. They doled out the fish slowly so that there was still some left mixed with the various fauna and some roots and the skin bags.

Whenever he stopped, he'd have some observation about what he'd seen or that it looked like it would be a clear night with not much wind. Not much wind was good. Clear nights were bitterly cold though. When Reece's hands started to hurt from cutting up Boo Boo she started to make the drying frames they'd designed by weaving flexible green thin branches. All this had been left within arm's reach.

Reece knew that if she wasn't so occupied with working with Jake to stay alive, she would be only above to focus on the extreme pain of her thigh. She looked at it once and shuddered. She knew she would not be walking in three days. The plan would be that she could hobble enough to get to a better place to rest and wait until she could walk again. She didn't know how long that would be, but she hoped it wouldn't be so long that they would have chewed though all of Boo Boo which would make the whole episode close to pointless. By nightfall there were some big piles of Boo Boo bits mounding up and plenty left to cut.

'Boo Boo was carrying a few pounds.' She pointed to the pile of yellow fat.

'He couldn't afford those pills they have for that these days.' He replied.

'Hell. If people want to lose weight come and do this for a few weeks.' After a moment she said. 'I was thinking maybe if we dipped some sticks in it, they might burn a bit when we're trying to ask nicely if the wolves wouldn't mind not eating us.'

Jake was nodding. 'A good idea. And you know. We could tie some fur to the end and really load them up with fat.'

This gave them both a very satisfying mind picture. They knew the wolves were going to be a major problem. And they would probably arrive soon. Now Reece was thinking of an additional strategy. 'And what if we brought them right in close? So we can nail them.'

Jake was a little uncertain about this until he heard the details.

They were both exhausted, but Jake had taken over some cutting while Reece divided her time between making wolf torches and weaving drying racks for Boo Boo meat.

They were sitting behind low walls of firewood with gaps between. However, they would only light them up, some fat smeared on the wood, if it was absolutely necessary. For all the fact they had been eating most of the day, they were still hungry and commenced the process of migrating large mound of meat from Boo Boo into a soft jerky.

'Pretty sure Caribou are an endangered species.'

Reece nodded. 'We learned about endangered species in biology. From what I could tell, it's pretty much all of them.'

'Yeah the world's screwed. The problem poor Boo Boo ran up against is he was less endangered than us.'

The laughter at this was a little grim. Reece didn't need to, but she wanted to say it. 'Hey. Thanks for not treating me like a dumb kid.'

Jake turned and looked her in the eye. 'Anyone who treats you that way Reece. Well. They don't know people. And they're not worth even a minute of your time. We got a tough night ahead of us but what do we do when life thinks it's going to push us around.'

'We get together and we kick its ass Cowboy.'

An hour later they heard the first howls.

They'd never been trying to protect such a big pile of fresh meat with so little firewood. Usually they had a ring of trees on fire around them which kept most unwelcome visitors away. They were anxious. But there was also an air of anticipation about taking on a pack of wolves. They had considered strapping the knife to a picket, but they simply could not risk it getting stuck in the wolf that got away.

The wolves came in and made their careful assessments of the danger and the reward. The leader of the pack could use his incredible sense of smell to measure the reward. The danger was fire. But it was much smaller than usual when they shadowed these two strange animals.

So they started to come in. And would chance the gaps between the piles still unlit. However something unexpected happened. It started to rain meat. The off cuts of Boo Boo came down towards what the person throwing them believed to be the lower end of the pack hierarchy. This did not make for a happy boss dog. Meat was then landing as much as possible at an equal distance between two wolves. This started to cause some unseemly disagreements within the pack. And it caused a dangerous lack of attention as to what the source of that meat was up to. Reece was lighting up their two heavy spears. They had a band of fur completely saturated in Boo Boo fat. It was tied on six inches behind the sharp point so this could still drive into flesh in front of the flame.

Jake calmed his nerves and waited while Reece threw out more of the off cuts. Then he walked quickly towards the snarling snapping pack. He'd held the spears pointed backwards away for the wolves along his forearms, so the flames were behind him until he was ready. He was going to take his time with the first one and try to make it count. He swung one spear up and sideways until it was pointing forward and drove it towards the target moving the least. He hit a wolf on the haunches as it was turning so it didn't penetrate. He got a yelp but that was all.

He was already swinging out the second pike. The flame was reducing quickly. This time he picked a target and walked out following it and drove the spear right behind the foreleg and in front of the rib cage. This dog made an indescribable noise. Jake and Reece weren't sure what would happen next. She had thrown some more off cuts.

The wolves were in confusion. There was food raining down on them, they were fighting over it, and one of their number must have come off badly in the fight. The flaming spears had not set any coats ablaze although there was the smell of singed fur. 'Come on Cowboy. Light one up for me.' She was laughing. They knew there was still a chance the predators could focus on them and decide to attempt a killing frenzy. They were ready to jump in the water and start swimming.

'Need more fuel for that. He dashed out and picked up the closest spear and Reece got it blazing. He reached down and took a big handful of the yellow congealing fat. If he got there when they were still in a frenzy he might just do it. He came out quickly. Risked losing a hand and threw the handful of fat on the back of a wolf and only pushed the flaming spear down on its back rather than throw it.

He knew it probably wouldn't take but he held the flaming fur torch on the place as best he could as the animal spun around. He'd held it for too long though. And although the flame started to take, the wolf figured out the source of its discomfort and was about to drive forward at him. Suddenly a light spear glanced off its muzzle leaving a deep cut. Reece was standing next to Jake with the crutch he'd made. The dogs were realising there was some unknowable force at work. Jake flung the spear as the entire pack turned as one to flee. He hit one an inch to the right of the tail which created a big yelp. It was funny to see the one which he'd lit up bounding in the distance. And the faster it ran the more oxygen there was to feed the flames. They were pumped with adrenaline and the wolves were treated to quite a bit of name calling as they fled.

They both expected to find at least one dead wolf. The second pike Jake threw should have punctured the animals heart. The bloody pike was found by the light of a Boo Boo torch. They were sure it would die. But they couldn't afford to look for it.

'The one skin I really wanted. Not the burnt one of course.' Said Reece.

'I'd nail that one to my wall.' Jake said as they walked back.

'Tell people about the time I set a wolf on fire with caribou fat and a handmade spear. Who's going to top that at a dinner party.'

'You have dinner parties.'

'I certainly would if I had a burned wolf skin on my wall. I'd only invite one person. And she saved me from getting bitten by the damn dog so I couldn't exaggerate as I might like to.'

'I finally get an invite to the ranch. Only had to spear a flaming wolf to get it.' For the first time, not only during this adventure, but in all their encounters previously, usually unsatisfyingly brief from Reece's perspective, there was a moment of serious awkwardness.

'Um…yeah.'

Reece smiled a smile of apology for raising it and moved on. 'How long before we hit the road again. If we take turns staying up, we should be out of here the day after tomorrow.'

Jake thought that optimistic but there was nothing to be gained in suggesting that. 'Sounds good. We'd be all rested up and have a big bag of Boo Boo. How's the fetlock.'

'I'll be ready to run a marathon by then.'

Jake knew she was in a great deal of pain, especially when there was nothing to focus on. 'Maybe I'll sleep and you manage the racks until…'

'I'm so exhausted I'll go to sleep in spite of the agony.'

'It's the only pain medication we have left. We had to be raided by a bear that was a painkiller junkie.'

She nodded. Then Jake looked across at her beaming and she said. 'You and me. We took on a pack of hungry wolves and had them running and yelping within five minutes.'

'They had no idea who they were up against.'

'I'll wake you up when I can't keep my eyes open.'

All the next day they worked on drying meat. They ate anything in their bags that was getting old as well as grilled fresh Caribou. Jake came back with a few roots and some greens but soon there would be few of those as the temperatures were falling and they knew the snowfalls would be heavy enough soon to cover the ground permanently. While collecting firewood Jake kept an eye out until he found the perfect shape. A long sturdy stick with a bend at the end which he could tie some skin to and make a better crutch.

Reece started moving around and got good at using it and not letting her injured leg touch the ground and she could move almost as fast as before. She was relieved that they would not need to stay a minute longer than necessary. On the second night they moved a little way off and let the wolves have all the bones and head and other parts that they couldn't use. Jake used the sinews as strings and the broken-up antlers were strapped tightly to sticks to be shoved in a wolf's face if they attacked. Reece loved this weapon, partly because it was; 'A cooler Wizards Staff then I ever saw Gandalf with '

Two days later they were relieved to be on the move, both with heavy skin packs full of food and ready to kill anything they could to preserve their supplies.

As they moved Jake keep looking until he found a perfect set of antlers from the remains of an elk to improve Reece's 'Staff of Justice'. It had been young animal, and a section of the antlers formed a tight upward facing bunch of a dozen spikes which he used the stone to sharpen to deadly points They were twisted by somehow balanced, and he took special care binding them to a shaft he believed was the right weight. Jake always carried his heavy spear and the best stone he could find.

Reece had her new staff for things that broke through the heavy spear's defences and a stone in her pocket because one hand would be on the crutch for a while.

A week later they were hit by a blizzard the like of which they had no experience of and realised they were completely ill equipped for. It came in quickly. Through the autumn they had various hints from the climate and the wildlife that bad weather was coming. They'd find an overhang, make a shelter, maintain a fire if they could or wait out what had as often been rain than snow. Which had never covered the ground for more than a day.

Suddenly everything around them was white. And it was a white that was stinging their eyes and hands and finding its way mercilessly though the layers of clothing and skins they wore. It had been Jake's turn to be wrapped in Boo Boo. He knew from the outset if he wanted Reece's respect one thing he had to observe was complete equality. He was attuned to her enough to know that if he suggested she should have more food, more warmth, a better piece of whatever fare they were eating or a better place to lie down in a cave or shelter it would be an insult to her and worse, a disappointment. They were in this together. So they took turns wrapping themselves in the best hide they had.

Jake had come up with several approaches to improve the curing process so Boo Boo was clean and supple. When the white out hit, he opened his arms and brought Reece into the biggest, warmest hide they had. They stood until they had to sit in the snow and hold each other tight. They thought they were inured to cold. But nothing like this. Both hoped a storm of this intensity wouldn't last long. But it did.

It had hit late morning. By mid-afternoon it had abated only slightly. They had said little. 'We won't survive the night sitting here Reece. We need to be behind some shelter and still trap the body heat. It's why they build igloos.'

He liked her so much because in this extremity, her leg still painful, shivering so that it affected her speech she could say. 'You can build an igloo.'

'Give me some solid ice, a saw and half dozen Innuit who know how to build an igloo and it'll be finished around the time the sun comes out in a few days.'

'Damn. I left the Innuit in my other pants along with the cave people.'

'Looks like it's us against a storm. Like a pack of wolves in a different way right.'

'Let's kick this storms ass.' Things didn't go well. They tried to walk together wrapped in Boo Boo but had to relent and take turns. Which needed to be short. They were in lightly wooded country with no variability in the terrain to shelter against and little dead wood to build from. As they walked, they realised how much they had to thank Boo Boo for. Each time they exchanged his coat they took a piece of his dried flesh and put it their mouth. They would never dream of chewing it. They sucked on it like it was a hard candy they wanted to savour as long as possible.

Finally they almost walked into a large dead tree on the ground. Not a great deal of cover but the position of the tree at least had one side in the lee of the wind and the other a solid drift of snow. They had to create an air pocket around themselves. They cut their hands breaking off as many dead branches on that tree and any others they could find to make a lean-to shelter. Before it was finished, they would retreat to it for a ten-minute interval to get out of the wind and steel themselves for more of the icy blasts. They found a good source of wood and came back with armfuls only to find they had lost their bearing to the tree. They wandered for an hour as the gloom of the evening stole around them much earlier in these conditions. Reece felt her foot fall into soft snow. They had walked over it.

Buried in snow as they had wandered around looking for it. They set their bags and Boo Boo aside and gave everything they had to rebuilding the shelter, pulling it apart digging out a space nearly to the frozen ground to give themselves what they hoped was the right amount of space to trap the heat but not have too much cold air to try to warm. Jake dumped all the food they had, frozen solid, inside the space and used the knife to cut open their skin carry bags and threw one over the sticks to form a better ceiling followed by a thick layer of pine tree browse on the roof and the floor. The activity had warmed them a little so Reece was followed suit as best she could. They brought pine tree brows for one side of the lean to and then packed a snow wall against them on the outside. They did this on part of the other side, leaving a hole to crawl into and covered the opening with the other skin.

They knew it would be more insulated inside. However, the temperatures were about to plummet. They arranged the clothing and skins the best they could. And holding each other tight wrapped themselves in Boo Boo. Doing nothing and being freezing cold was the worst. They were too cold to sleep even though they were exhausted. Reece's leg had been punished far too soon to be doing that kind of work. She was crying.

But was doing so quietly, she was sure Jake didn't hear it over the storm. He did know. He was crying also. From exhaustion and the first ever feeling of despair. That they might not make it. And he would lose her. As it continued, they decided they needed to burn energy to keep warm, so they ate as much of their dwindling supply as they wanted and began to flex their muscles, the other wrapped in Boo Boo. They did this for hours until their muscles ached, but they knew it was keeping them, and the air around them warmer.

Sometimes conditions like that can last days. Had it done so they would have perished. The warm sunshine melted their ceiling, and it was the dripping of water that woke them. They quickly gathered up the dried meat before it thawed out and turned to mush in a pile. They crawled out and sat in the sun and said nothing for a long time.

'That was rough.' Said Jake.

'Yep.'

'I don't want to do that again.'

Reece's laughed. 'I'm with you there.'

She liked that what he said next was a real question. Not something he went through before presented his own idea. 'So what do we do?'

They sat in the sunshine for fifteen minutes. Thawing out and thinking. Cowboy's question had opened the floor. Either of them might pose a solution. There was no solution, there was a decision on what they could try do to survive as winter threatened to overwhelm them.

'Sounds obvious but I think we've got to get the hell out of here.' Said Reece. 'I think our only hope is to change our tactics and move as fast as we possibly can to get somewhere there are people. Or maybe if we came across an abandoned cabin we might make it. But I have no idea how anything lives through the winters here. Hibernation isn't an option for us unfortunately.'

Jake was nodding as she spoke. He said nothing for a while and then. 'Can't see any other way. We should only try and catch something if it's close to a sure thing and worth the investment in energy. I think we'll be worn out come mid-afternoon. Should be on the lookout all day for places to shelter in case we get hit by a storm like that, even if we have to back track to it, so we don't have to try to build a shelter in the middle of one.'

'I'm with you there. Maybe if we need to decide which way to walk we chose the path that could provide shelter.' She nodded and rarely for Reece, she repeated something. 'Yeah. That was…rough.'

He looked across and smiled. 'We're all warmed up. Food's ready to pack and all we have to do is get ourselves into a gallop for the last…'

'Thousand miles?'

He laughed. 'I have absolutely no idea how far that plane flew and…hell, winters are cold on the ranch and that's at least a few thousand miles south of here. I thought we'd be back easily by four months. Exactly like you say Reece. We've got to do the equivalent of a sprint from now on. Remembering we wouldn't be here if we hadn't stopped for the No I-Deer and Boo Boo and all the others. But they aren't around anymore.'

'So let's go.'

They hadn't walked in deep snow for a whole day before and irrespective of their intention to move quickly, it was demoralising to be making less progress than they were accustomed to while using twice the energy. There were more lakes to navigate, and it was a guessing game to travel east or west around them.

In the afternoon they saw a low ridge to the east. It was in rocky country so they followed it and it continued some distance into a lightly forested area. They were exhausted so they set up a fire next to a good emergency shelter. They tried to light up a few trees, but the air temperature was too cold and they were birch trees which lacked the oils of the pine and cedars. Hence the fire was less than they would have liked it to be. It was nice to get back to back as they usually did. There was no longer any question of taking turns to stay awake. They would have to respond to the wolves when they were woken up by them. Although they did both start to suspect their minds where acclimatising to their circumstances. They would wake up if there was a strange noise. Maybe an inquisitive fox or a pile of snow sliding off a tree.

They were burning so much energy they simply had to eat more than they knew was sustainable. They decided to eat all the days rations in one session when the stopped to make camp. They would eat, get warm and, if the weather was kind, get rest. They walked on a low ridge and were relieved it was only covered by a few inches of snow and cut south through the many lakes. There was some broken ground to navigate but they were able to start to move much faster than they ever had.

However the weight was shedding from around their bones. They knew their bodies were burning muscle now to keep them alive which was soon going to be a vicious cycle.

They came upon a scene that would once have made them run in the other direction. Now it was only a glance and they were leaping forward as they did in the caribou hunt. A pack of wolves had brought down an Elk after hiving it from the herd and stalking it through the night. The senior members of the pack had been tearing into it for an hour. But it was a big animal. Considerably bigger than Boo Boo.

Jake carried the heavier pike. The same which had gone into the neck of Boo Boo and later pierced a wolf that certainly died of the injury. The other pike had a burned tip and hence was weakened, so irrespective of the sentimental attachment Jake had developed for it, it had to be left behind. He couldn't carry two. He was going to put it on a fire but Reece said it was. 'A noble weapon that doubtless slayed its foe.' It was left on a ledge in a cave. He could barely throw the one he carried now. When they saw the size of the animal on the ground, they were suddenly galvanised. That elk was the only thing that was going to keep them alive. They were going to fight to the death for it.

They didn't yell on the way in.

Some of the animals lower in the pack waiting for the hierarchy to have their fill saw them coming and paced about nervously however there were no precedents to draw on in terms of responses. The two bipeds were suddenly among them wreaking havoc and confusion and very quickly mortal injuries. Their stone throwing was pathetic. Reece threw too early and missed. Jake, who might have killed a wolf a few weeks ago, got a yelp from a hit to the foreleg and a limping dog.

One wolf got a viscous jab in the face from a dozen sharpened antlers with the next already lined up. Jake would not chance a throw. They would have to get in close to win this prize. With strength he would not have guessed he had left Jake drove the pike into the flank of a wolf so hard it pierced right through the rib cage. Now they were yelling. Screaming at the wolves that this was their piece of meat. They started to make references to their appearance and the likely deficiencies of their wolf relatives. Neither used much in the way of profanity out of respect for the other but also the partnership. One dog lay dead another dying from desperate pike thrusts, four others with nasty wounds to the face and another limping badly. Half of the pack had some kind of injury from the altercation. They fled followed by various versions of 'And don't come back.'

Both knew they would come back. Or others. There wasn't much around in the way food and many animals, like them, needed to risk all to survive. Reece and Jake knew they were too far from the timber to do what they did with Boo Boo and they didn't believe they could afford to stop. Even to put on condition. The skin was ruined as a blanket and they would not be able to skin it with the knife now so notched and blunt. However there were large sections of the carcass barely touched.

Cowboy looked at Reece. He let her say it if it needed to be said. So she knew she was never the kid and he the experienced old man. 'Take what we can carry?' She said.

'I'll start cutting it into lumps.' It was mid-morning. 'Do you think we take a day and eat as much as we can and then carry as much as we can?'

'I'll go down to the tree line and set things up.' She said. It was rare now for them to separate but they had to take risks. And there was no way she would sit by while Cowboy worked frantically. He checked the horizon to see if the wolves had regrouped or were slinking around. There was no sign of them. Reece went to the elk and stroked it's much abused neck. 'Thanks for saving us.' She was exhausted and got emotional easily now, so she turned away.

Then she went to two dead wolves and said. 'Thanks for not killing us.' They were now both sorry to have wrought so much damage on animals with motivations identical to their own and wondered if they could have tempered their attack.

'Did we act like crazy people?'

'Yeah.'

She went to the younger of the two and said. 'If only there was time we could at least take the hide and I could have been Wolf Girl.'

'You may not be Wolf Girl but in my version of American Indian parlance you're. Girl who makes wolves afraid.'

'I'll take that. I'll come back once things are set up and start carrying some down. It might get waved over the fire briefly because I'm getting to like my steak rare.'

Exhausted and hungry as she was, she was gratified to be able to choose a place she thought was the best for them to shelter for the night, build it, collect some firewood and then get back to Jake and carry a load of meat over. The wolves were now slinking around on the margins, and they were unsure about whether to chance another encounter.

The knife was hardly functioning so Jake had cut some very untidy, but large lumps of flesh off, and tried to take pieces of undamaged hide with them. Every little bit of fur was useful. Even though it added to the aroma of the poorly cured skins of six species. They shoved some of it in their boots now to keep warm but also stop them sliding off. He'd cut more than they could both carry in one trip.

Reece couldn't carry anything like the load Jake could with her leg healing only slowly with all the demands being put on it. She said. 'Girl who make wolves afraid can fend them off for half an hour. You'll see my tracks. There's a tree you can put the meat in right near the shelter. A pine tree. So we might light that sucker up if it doesn't snow on us.'

Jake didn't play at needing to be convinced for her to take a risk. He picked up the heavy bag, picked up his pike and started walking as quickly as he could. Had the wolves broken to follow him she would have called him back. However the wolves knew where the main course was. Hunger was biting at them. They would wait for darkness.

The exhaustion was starting show when Jake returned. Clothing and furs tied on with sinews that used to fit snugly were now hanging from both. The elk was lifesaving, but they were not going to be able to eat enough and have enough range of foods to get into condition to continue the walk for weeks. They had to keep moving in the hope of finding people or some situation like a summer hunting cabin where they could try to survive the rest of the winter.

They didn't let that dampen the joy of eating as much as they wanted. When that joy had passed, they went through the somewhat less joyful experience of continuing to eat. They even forced themselves to swallow little frozen beads of elk fat so they didn't need to chew it. The meat didn't need to be smoked to carry because it was frozen solid the next morning and even carrying it, it never got below a cold refrigerator temperature. Though it did soak their backs with bloody elk juice They had more than they could carry the next day. They knew where the wolves were, they'd listened to them all night arguing over the order via which they would fill their bellies. She heard some sounds that might have been very young dogs. Pups old enough for their first outing. They could have both slept through the night but took turns. Not to watch, but to toast and eat small quantities, preparing some for the other while they slept.

That night Reece said. 'I never want to see another piece of elk meet again. Boo Boo was way better.'

'No problem. What's for breakfast?'

'Elk meat. Which is way better than no meat.'

'I do dream of plates full of vegetables when I sleep.'

'In a sauna.'

'We will have walked right up to a big resort with a sauna by late this afternoon and ask for the menu. Vegetarian please.'

'We'll probably get arrested for wearing rare and endangered fauna.'

'We may need to take some care about that at the Reception Desk.'

'We'll need to hide the wolf pup I plan to go and wrest away from the pack when they attack us again. Do they eat much.'

'Not too much. But I might eat the puppy when you're not looking.'

'Damn. No wolf pup. My only chance to be the cool girl at school.'

'Those people don't need to find out about the fact you land planes on ice fields, light up forests, kill caribou with a stick and see off wolf packs. Twice. That's how little they matter. You're the cool girl to me.'

She looked across and smiled. 'That matters.'

There was no resort. There were nights they could light some of the forest up around them to get truly warm.

There were days when it snowed heavily with barely any wind. And when their food was nearly gone, they were caught in a blizzard for two days and two night and came out with nothing left to carry. Even though it wasn't weather they would usually walk in, windy with sleet, they knew unless they left what had turned into an ice cave, they would never get out of it. The wind had died down in the afternoon and there was a light snowfall which would have been welcome where they lived. Memories of which were becoming patchy as their brains competed for blood with the arms and legs they forcing to move. They were in a light woodland of pine and spruce and it thinned out towards a clearing. It was Jake's turn to be wrapped in Boo Boo.

They hadn't had much to say since they left the shelter. If they could light up some trees they might make another night, or two. But getting things to take light quickly while flicking the lighter flame on for only a second was almost impossible now. They carried any fuel they found but had not found anything suitable that day and they had run out of elk fat to help things light.

Reece looked into the clearing through the trees and squinted. 'Do you get mirages in the snow.'

'I don't know. Do you see…what is it…sand dunes and a pool of water and date palms.'

It was essential they didn't crumble. Now. At last. At the end of the Odessey. 'No.'

'Damn. I wouldn't care if it was real or not. I'd love to see that.'

'How about white tents covered in snow.' Her voice was rising with relief and excitement.

It was the same for him as the structures came into focus. A big fireplace surrounded by rocks in front the cluster of tents. 'Is it surrounded by date palms.'

'Yeah Cowboy. Date palms everywhere.' She was laughing and then started crying from relief and exhaustion. He opened up Boo Boo and wrapped them together. Jake was reacting the same way. Except his mind kept sending up two words for him to examine. White tents.

They heard a voice behind them. 'What in the fuck do we have here.' Three men had been walking behind them at a distance for five minutes. 'It's like Robinson Crusoe and Girl Friday.'

Jake didn't like the voice and in particular the way the speaker said; Girl. They were completely covered in the skin and Jake leaned in to say. 'Wolves.'

They weren't going to react based on a tone of voice but they were wary creatures now. Jake slid the bottom of the pike backwards so it was kept concealed by Boo Boo. Reece did the same with the Staf of Justice. Jake only lowered Boo Boo to above their shoulders so the men following couldn't see what they held.

'I have spent most of my life in the wilds and I've never come across anything like this. What are you; the people that were raised by wolves.' Said the man who had spoken first. He was carrying a gun.

Reece smiled. 'Yeah.'

'Seems the rest of the pack aren't with you right now so why don't you come over and get warm. Looks to me that you haven't had much to eat lately. Maybe something hot to drink.'

Jake would test the man. Though it was a huge test for himself to refuse what was offered 'Friend. I spend most of my life roaming around countryside similar to this. So we've got that much in common. We very much appreciate the offer. But my friend and I…we're only passing through. We finally got in touch with some people we know and we're meeting them not too far from here. I can tell you we're looking forward to seeing them. Been a pleasure though.'

Reece gave no hint of the fact that she would be following Cowboy's lead the instant they got their answer.

The man's voice hardened. 'There aren't any people not too far from here mister and I'd appreciate it if you'd comply with my friendly welcome...or this will be more of a situation where...you do what I fucking tell you to do.' His gun started to lift from where he'd had it pointing down for his initial 'welcome'.

'I think we understand that now.' Said Reece.

It was easier for Reece to make a fast jab to the man's face than it was for Jake to bring up his pike and drive it forward. He was watching Reece. She hit the man who'd been speaking to them first. He was completely taken by surprise and staggered back. She'd pulled back and rammed the staff topped with the cluster of sharp antler spikes it into the face of the man next to him, with, it turned out, much greater effect. He staggered back and threw his head into his hands. Jake drove the pike into the third man's stomach, but he had too many layers of clothes on and he was a very big man. He got over the surprise quickly was reaching down to grab the pike but it slid out of his hands with the residue of Boo Boo's fat making it a little slippery.

Jake aimed again. And as with their attack on the wolves, he was certain their lives depended on it and he stepped forward driving the pike hard up under the man's chin. I may have been less effective however the man had pulled his arm back, bunched his fist and was stepping forward to deliver a blow which might have snapped Jake's neck. The pike came out the back of his head. When Jake tried to pull it out, he ended up pulling the man onto him. The pike was wedged against a tree and drove right through. At that same moment Reece had refocused and stepped forward with the antler topped shaft to drive it into the first man's face again. The first strike had made some nasty puncture wounds but hadn't driven into an eye as with the man next to him.

He was going to bring up the rifle and empty the magazine into both of them but she was fast. He had to react by pushing the shaft across with one hand to stop another driving blow. There was more force behind it then he realised, and he could only push it sideways as an antler barely missed his eye and scraped a channel across the side of his cheek and tore into the top of his ear. She was barely able to stop her own momentum as the weapon glanced off its target.

Jake had allowed the big man to slump down and roll to the side and reached out and clasped Reece by the shoulder and pulled her. 'Come on. Run Reece. We've got to run.' She held her staff, but they left Boo Boo and the pike.

The only man standing now had instinctively put his hand up to his ear. Blood was coming down from his forehead and brows. He hadn't lost an eye, but the man next to him had. He was screaming and had fallen to his knees. 'Fuck. My fucking eye.'

The man with the gun wiped the blood from his face but there was so much he initially smeared more into them. He pulled his jacket up roughly and wiped his face which hurt because he was pulling open the scratches and four deep puncture wounds. It didn't help his vision enough, so he unzipped his jacket and pulled up his undershirt and pressed it into his eyes. Blood was going to tricked back into them so he lifted the rifle and took a shot and missed. He'd been aiming for the girls head. Then two thoughts stuck him. One was that the boss was going to want them alive to find out what they knew and if anyone else knew where they were. And also he wanted to keep them alive; because she was going to pay.

It was pathetic to watch them run. They were among the trees, appearing only occasionally between them.

They thought they'd escaped. He'd been shooting game in the forest since he was seven. He brought the man down with a shot to the leg by which time his eyes again had blood running into them. He saw her crouch down, so he ran towards them.

Jake went down on his shoulder and slid a little through the snow. Reece was beside him trying to get him to stand within seconds. He was reaching into the pouch at the inside of the skin vest he wore over the old burned jacket. He handed her the knife. Holding the blade and pushing the hilt towards her. 'Please Please Reece. Don't argue. Run. You have to run.'

She looked and saw the man coming. She shared a glance with Jake. There was nowhere for her to go. There was no chance of her surviving more than a few nights even if it was mild. Especially without Boo Boo. She knew Jake was telling her it would be better for her not to be caught as that could be worse than dying of exposure.

The Reece who first learned retaliation in childcare started to emerge in that moment. She came close to his ear. 'Be ready for anything.' Anger caught alight in her mind in that second. Her parents were exposed to some of her ability to contrive outcomes that suited her.

As had those that thought she was fodder for bullying. She had a great deal more of this trait she had never tapped into. She turned and ran. And she knew now not to run in a straight line. She was running towards heavier woods but they were still a way off. The man arrived at where Jake lay.

'Tell her to stop and she won't need to get shot.' Reece's running was nothing like the energy they had chasing Boo Boo. She was staggering and using her shaft to stop her falling occasionally. The shooter was wiping his eyes again. 'Okay.' He said.

Jake was lying a few yards from him and was able to roll over quickly as the man was taking aim and drive the arch of his foot hard from his position lying on his side into the side of the shooter's knee. The shot went well high as he cried out in pain. He turned around and slammed the rifle butt into Jakes head. The gunman's face was drenched in blood, he was overtaken by a fury which had rarely hit this mark, even for a man prone to anger. He let a monumental shout of frustration. 'Fuuuuuck.' He tore his jacket and shirt off, then his vest, put the outer layers back on and pressed his face into the thermal for a few minutes to try to stem the bleeding. Jake was unconscious.

A man arrived, running through the deep snow. 'Chess what's...'

'Shut up. Just shut up. Drag this piece of shit to the camp and tie him up.'

A man with an ex-military bearing said. 'Bertram's screaming and Davey's, shit he's…'

'I know. You think I don't know that. Drag him to the camp and get Claude to bring Bertram in. Is Kirk finished yet?'

'We looked in. He's still on a call. Waved us off. We better let him…'

He looked up to see another man standing back at where the trio had been attacked. 'Yeah. I know that too alright. I know that too. You guys do what I've asked; twice now and I'll see Kirk.'

The other man who had arrived was looking at the big man laying dead in disbelief. He finally turned to Bertram. Chess was now walking past. Taking no interest in the dead, injured or disbelieving. 'What the fuck have you done Chess.'

'For Christ sake Claude, will you bring him in.' He wasn't looking forward to the meeting he was about to have but it would be worse if someone else let Kirk know and the boss came looking for him to get explanations.

He saw the two skin bags the travellers were carrying next to the caribou skin and he picked them up to take to Kirk.

The ex-medic came back and said. 'Claude. There's a man unconscious back there. Do you think you can drag him in I'll get Betram in and start treating him.'

'Okay Doc.' Claude said this in a daze, as Doc took Bertram's arm. The French Canadian was looking down at what was had been a big but usually gentle and soft-spoken man who was more likely than not to get people laughing. 'What the fuck just happened Doc.' He said quietly

'Only that… idiot Chess can tell us Claude. Call out if you need help.'

Chess knocked and opened the door. A man who had been interrupted three times now on the weekly call looked around ready to bite someone's head off this time. Then he saw Chess's face. 'Gentlemen, Vanessa; I have to attend to something. Vanessa if you could gather up any questions for me and send them through and we'll schedule another call when it suits you all and I'll address them and we can get through the rest of the items on the agenda.'

Chess took note the fact that Kirk had not the slightest trace of concern or sympathy in his voice, as he might have done for anyone else in the camp. 'What did that to your face?'

You're supposed to be in camp working in the processing room. Not chasing something you spotted on surveillance.'

Chess let out a long slow breath and pressed his face into his vest again. 'We saw some people walking this way who triggered a trail camera. Davey, Bertram and I went out to find out who they were.'

'You saw people. We don't get people here. That's why we're here. How can there be people coming towards our operations and I don't know about that immediately.'

'You waved us off. You were on the phone.'

'I wave people off when they have routine shit they get paid enough to figure out for themselves and if they can't do that I fuck them off. This is something you interrupt about because…' Kirk was wasting his own time now. His dislike for Chess had been growing steady and he could see this was going to probably cross a threshold he knew was coming in their future when he first met the man. 'I heard two shots. Rifle practice I'd assumed. Is that how you managed this Chess. And then what. Put you face in front of a bear.'

'Well shit Kirk maybe if you weren't so busy listening to the sound of your own fucking voice I could have told you what happened by now.'

'You're right Chess.' Vanessa; the organisation's bookkeeper's was the bosses stepdaughter and had a brother who was not his choice for the team.

'We walked up to these two people. Friendly. Asked them what they were doing here. Been wandering around for months by the look of them. I invited to them to the camp and they pulled out these…weapons they'd been hiding in a…skin.' Chess paused not to give Kirk and opportunity to say something but because he was trying to spin the attack as an unavoidable outcome.

'Go on.'

'The girl jabbed me in the face with this, stick that had a cluster of antlers tied to it. I hadn't been expected anything like that and by the time I figured out what was going on she'd done the same to Bertram. Then the older guy, he had this, heavy sharpened spear thing and, I couldn't see properly because I had to fend off the antlers coming at me again, but it looks like he hit Davey in the throat. I pushed the antler thing out of the way before it hit me in the face again. The old guy grabbed her and they started running. My God damn eyes were full of blood so it…'

'Hold up a minute.'

'Did you say girl.'

'Yeah the one with the antler thing was a girl. I don't know she'd be sixteen maybe. They're both scrawny as fuck. The skins they'd made were hanging off them.'

'Chess. Are you telling me you're not the only one who got injured in an altercation with a scrawny girl and another 'old guy'.'

Chess was a little annoyed by this but also anxious to make the clarifications he was about to. 'Like I said. They had two weapons hidden and they attacked us with no warning and for no reason.'

'We'll get back to that. Davey and Bertram. They can still do their jobs right. We can't afford to be short-handed at this time of year. And Bertram is the specialist who should have been in the place he is paid to do that work. This isn't the kind of operation where we take people to a hospital. Which is where you won't be going.'

Chess would eventually have to reveal he had gone to get Bertram and Davey to come with him. Bertram was not the logical choice, however they were the two that were less likely to challenge his suggestion that they go and 'check things out' rather than Claude, whom he despised, and Doc who thought he was better than everyone because he had a military background. He didn't bother to try to soften it.

'From what I saw Betram got hit pretty bad. Lost an eye maybe. Davey's…gone.'

This solicited quite a pause. 'Gone?'

'The fuckers killed him. A big heavy sharpened pole under his chin. Came out the back of his head.'

Kirk was incredulous. 'Davey's dead and Bertram's blind. You could have fucking led with that you moron.' He walked up to the man who was bigger than him and was already carrying a scar from a glass to the face in a fight in a bar. Now it would be scarred much more. 'A scrawny girl and some 'old guy' pick a fight for no reason. What did you say to them?' Kirk's anger was building. And it was much more controlled, but much more dangerous that Chess's.

'I said they should come and have something to eat and a hot drink at the camp.'

'And what did they say.'

'They made up some bullshit they were meeting people nearby and they wanted to be on their way.'

'And what did you say.'

'Kirk me and Clive could be out there tracking her down right now. I came to tell you what happened as soon as I got Doc and Claude to drag that fucker back here and get Bertram in. It'll be dark in an hour.'

Kirk ignored this. 'What did you say.'

'I told them that, more or less, it wasn't an option.'

'And then, they attacked you by surprise.'

'You can think what you like Kirk. I want to go and catch that fucking bitch to make sure she doesn't get away. You can tear strips off me as much as you like when I come back but…'

'A fucking 'scrawny bitch' is going to walk six hundred miles out of here is she Chess. We've got drones and tracking dogs and I'm going to call the field team back in. We aren't going to do anything until I've processed this…' He finished the sentence in a shout of frustration. '…fuck up. It's what intelligent people do Chess. They stop and think. It's not like she's going to get far. I assume Bertram's with Doc. Bring me this 'old guy' you caught.'

'He was out to it when I left him. I shot him in the leg but he…I hit him. Pretty sure he's alive though.'

'This is like water torture. Now I hear shooting him in the leg wasn't going to slow him down enough. I need to know what he knows. I need to know who else could possibly know where he is. What is wrong with you. I'm trying to figure out some way you might have fucked this up worse. Any details you've left out?'

Chess was becoming sour and tipping into the anger mode that made the glassing he got in a bar one price he'd paid for his behaviour over the years. 'You can say what the fuck you want but you had to be there.'

'I'll tell you where I was. I was talking to a bunch of people who are all getting more and more pissed off with a bookkeeper who is supposed to do administration work in a very delicate operation. But she's the fucking Owners stepdaughter and you're her brother. So I have to deal people that would never usually be involved in an operation like this.'

'From my recollection there would be no operation like this without us Kirk. Who took the Old Man out into this country years ago. Isn't that what led him to start all this up.'

Kirk was barely listening. What was happening to the operation was dawning on.

He walked in close. Menacing. 'I would have fought and struggled and eventually won the fight to get you out of this operation except for one reason. You're fucking dog. That animal is the best tracker and holding dog I've ever seen. It finds game that the drones don't pick up and then he holds it if it's injured and going to get away but barely leaves a mark. And he knows his limits. Chess you tell people in this operation, especially your stepfather about how much you bring in, well guess what. It's Clive that does all that. And you got that dog after your father picked him out of a litter and trained him.' Again Kirk caught himself wasting time to castigate Chess a little more, since this opportunity had presented itself for full disclosure.

'So go and get Doc to come and see me and then get your face treated and go and work with Claude in the processing room. Which is where you were supposed to be. And leave this disaster area to me.'

Chess was not unaccustomed to such appraisals, though the details might vary. He had spent so much time in the wilds pursuing various illicit activities because meetings like this usually marked the end of his forays into legitimate employment. Often finishing in violence or the threat of it. He would have done jail time if it weren't for his stepfather. Who had many interests, but one overriding passion.

Ironically that passions had been ignited by Chess when he took the 'Old Man' hunting when his stepdaughter encouraged him to get away from the city and come out to the place she'd spent time with their mother when she visited Chess occasionally. Chess's stepfather bought and sold beautiful things and used them as an entrée into the lives of the rich and powerful. And when he was shown the secrets of the wilderness and it's beautiful and dangerous wildlife it lit a fire. An ambition to take this variety of the rare and beautiful to those who would pay. And they invited him more and more into the world he had always wanted to inhabit but had no doorway to such a life available to him. Now he provided things to those who had everything. Almost. He supplied them with things which they could get nowhere else. And he had a team that travelled the world to do it. It kept these groupings of strange bedfellows in the wilderness together. This was the reason he didn't want his stepson, a growing inconvenience now, in jail or outside the tent. He even let him believe things to placate a bristling ego in a small mind.

When Doc arrived, his nick name an honorific from his time as a paramedic in the army, Kirk saw a man deeply concerned; indeed deeply troubled. Doc had seen plenty of traumatic injuries. He'd come here to get away from that.

Take advantage of the balm of nature to mitigate his PTSD. And the money was amazing. And it was working, though he realised more and more didn't like the business. And now things had gone into reverse.

'What's the damage Doc.'

'Betram. He's…one eye's mush, the other ones so badly scratched if he ever sees anything out of it again it won't be much. Davey. Christ.' He exhaled as a brief ironic laugh. 'I'm used to bullet wounds and IED's. It's like a cave man jammed a big spear under his chin and right through the back of his head. I have no idea what it was that did that to Bertram's face. And you've seen Chess.'

'About Chess. When you treat his wounds, I want you to find something…I don't know what. Dogshit. Smear some in there. I want that fucker's face to get so infected he dies in agony while I'm around to watch.'

Doc smiled. 'Yeah we'd all like to do that Kirk…'

Kirk's voice was flinty. 'I'm not joking Doc. He's got half a dozen puncture wounds. Get six different things that have a good chance of getting infected and squeeze one each in there. And that's all I ever want to hear about him.'

'Can we treat Bertram here. I realise there's no chance of him getting back to the taxidermy now. We'll be losing some stock until I can replace him.'

Doc was surprised. Kirk saw this mainly as a human resources problem. He'd line up replacements for Davey, Bertram and Chess apparently and get back to work.

'This is a medivac situation Kirk. I can't treat him. I'm not a doctor I'm a field paramedic. I've done the first responder part. He was hysterical when I brought him in, and I can't image the pain he's in. I've used up quite a bit of what we have on the shelf to calm him down. The stocks are a bit more depleted than they should be.' Kirk could imagine the cause of that. 'We'll need to bring Davey in once I get everyone treated. That might need three of us he's so…big. Not sure if Chess will be up to it so I might need to come and get you.'

Kirk was impatient. 'Use the snowmobile.'

'Chess has the guts out of that. A 'service'.'

'Why the fuck am I the last to hear about these things. We always keep one in service on the base.'

Doc was rapidly getting over the whole place. He shrugged. 'You talk at people Kirk and don't listen to them so they give up trying to tell you things. Snowmobiles are nothing to do with me and the garage tent is twenty yards away. Why don't you get up and do a ten-minute inspection every day. That's what an effective manager would do. It's what I'm used to.' Doc was getting angry. A big friendly simple man was dead and another who loved taxidermy and was happy to share his enthusiasm for it was blind. And Kirk was bitching about a snowmobile not being available to recover a body. 'Oh yeah. And you have an asshole working here that also doesn't listen to anyone and steals the drugs from a locked cabinet. There's a few reasons Kirk. Pick one.' Doc was about to walk out.

Kirk let all that pass. He needed Doc and, unlike Chess, Kirk was a man who stored up his retaliation until it suited him organisationally. It was true Kirk wasn't much concerned about the fate of Davey. Betram was the problem. 'So can we keep Bertram…' He shrugged. '…stabilised for a while.'

Doc had dealt with plenty of brass, good and bad. He'd been known for being direct with them. Kirk was only an employer. Barely. 'Sorry I didn't explain it clearly enough to you Kirk. No. I can't.'

Kirk's voice had a sharp edge that needed to admit only a little sarcasm. 'Do you see a helicopter anywhere around here Doc. We're not in Iraq now.'

'Maybe there needs to be a helicopter Kirk because...'

'Because you want to go to fucking jail. Because you know so little about helicopters that we're outside the range of the nearest one that could get here. Because he'd be five days on a snowmobile. Camp at night? Do you see a magic wand on my desk Doc.'

'He is going to be in unbearable pain within days and I would give him less than a week without proper hospital care.'

'Thanks for giving me the situation report. Keep him comfortable.'

Kirk didn't seem much concerned about what happened once that was achieved. 'And?' Said Doc assuming there was some kind of alternative to the things that weren't going to happen.

'And that's my problem. I want to talk to the half of the partnership that has totally trashed our season.'

'He's unconscious.'

'So go and get some snow, put some water with it, make it into a slurry and throw it over him and see if that helps.'

'Kirk, I'm not comfortable…'

'I don't give a fuck about your degree of comfort Doc. We have everything to lose here. You know what you signed up for. And you might be afraid of the law Doc but I'm way more afraid of the people we work for. Because they make promises to people all around the world. Serious promises. People want the shit we acquire to give to their wives or mistresses, politicians, businessmen, Emirs or fucking presidents. And our supply chain has turned to shit. Now I need to speak to that person to understand if there is any chance that someone might know even roughly where those two are. And if they do, we might be breaking camp while being short on manpower. So wake him up and get him in here. If you don't like it, start fucking walking home Doc, but take nothing because you own nothing.'

Once Reece knew she wasn't being pursued she ran some more and was sitting in a tree trembling. If she made it through the night, it would be the last one. Apparently they thought the same because no one had followed her. She'd heard the dogs. It was laughable that she could even try to conceive a plan to get through so many people with guns and dogs to try to rescue Jake.

Only so they could get away until they were caught again or they die of exposure. Maybe that was the plan. Let her die of exposure. Do the same with Jake. They would leave them somewhere and the bears and wolves could tear them to pieces and if pieces were ever found it would look like what it was. They ran out of food and body heat.

'Wolves.' Jake had said. They usually kept out of their way. But when they had nothing to lose, the pair of wayfarers had taken risks. And the wolves had come off badly She had absolutely nothing to lose. She tensed every muscle in her body and forced herself to stop trembling, both from the cold and the fear. She had made a lifestyle out of outsmarting some people. Ideally not even allowing them to realise that's what she was doing. Because people looked at her and listened to what she chose to say and they believed what she wanted them to believe. There were the kind of people she liked and respected; they liked and respected her. This had included some teachers. One of them had said something that had always stayed with her. 'You'll never out power power Reece. You have to outsmart it.' She made her plan; and moved.

She realised she had to change the math. It was the only thing that could make anything else possible. She hoped her ideas weren't so obvious that they'd be waiting.

However, as night fell Kirk was distracted on many fronts. Otherwise he might have had enough suspicion to manage a low probability risk with simple surveillance. He was good at managing probable risks. Two scrawny wayfarers killing one of his workforce, maiming two more and destabilising the rest was not something that had been on his radar.

He walked out of the manager's cabin to see Chess leaving with his dog and gun.

'Are you retarded. I'm not even supposed to use that word but even the people who don't like it would apply it to you. What part of keep out of this did you not understand.'

'I'm the one trying to do the damage control Kirk. She can't be far away. Got nowhere to go. But if she dies tonight, we don't know what she knows. There could be people looking for these two and we need to find that out. I'll have her back here in under an hour.'

Initially Kirk thought Chess was probably right. The man they caught might not wake up or he may not talk whereas the girl might. At the same time his instincts were starting to tell him the way she came in, and what people believed about the way she left, was as important as bringing her in.

'Put your gun away and chain Clive up. If you disregard my instructions again Chess, everyone in this camp will be behind you. To run you down. And I'll ask that fucking scrawny girl with her magic staff to join us. Go and work in the processing room with Claude. We're short-handed. And get Doc to look at your face.'

Kirk knew he'd said enough. Sending Chess to work out here was the best compromise the Old Man could make to manage a potential security risk no matter how much Kirk bitched about it. However he had been getting hints from the Old man that if Chess suffered some kind of misadventure, it would be seen as an occupational hazard. Kirk's mind was starting to slide to a place where he might be the only one to make it out. All because of two improbable drifters. He entered the barracks. The small compound looked like it was comprised of tents. However, a few were prefabricated wooden panel structures. In winter they were covered in a white tent that fit over the structure. For the time they spent either side of the winter, they had a few other colours depending on where they'd set up the complex and how much cover they had.

When Kirk walked into the wood panel room that served as a barracks for six men, two always being out in the field Bertram asked who was there. Kirk couldn't say nothing, so he said he'd come to look in on him.

'I'm fucked up Kirk. I got pads and a bandage on my eyes.' His voice was breaking. 'I'm pretty sure my eyes are screwed. My eyes. They're my trade. How could this happen. One minute we're talking to some fucking weirdos and the next I get stuck with something with antlers tied to it. I got to get out of here. Doc's not a doctor. How are you going to get me out of here Kirk.'

'I'm working on it.'

'But how. The float plan can't get in and…'

Kirk was beginning to get very frustrated. In the space of an hour everything had turned to shit, and he didn't run operations that turned to shit. That's why they hired him 'I'm working on it. Give me some time. And don't keep on at me or I'll move you down the list. I'm dealing with a shit show here.'

Doc came in with a collapsable bucket with a little snow in the bottom and was going to add some water from a water bottle.

'What is it with you people.' Said Kirk irritably. 'Go and look after Chess's face.' Doc was nearly out the door when Kirk called to him. 'That guys leg? What the damage.'

'In and out. I've disinfected it and dressed it. A few stitches and some rest he'll be fine.'

'Good.' Doc thought it would cost nothing to add a thanks to that. Everyone else did. But not Kirk. Kirk followed him out the door and next to stores tent and filled the bucket with snow and went to the water tap connected to a tank which was kept inside to stop it from freezing. He mixed up a slurry and came back into the barracks. Bertram asked who it was.

'Is that you Davey.' Kirk wasn't going to be the one to put up with Bertram's reaction to that piece of news. The two worked closely on processing the merchandise. Davey would have been the only other one worth keeping from Kirk's new perspective.

'It's me.' Said Kirk. His tone conveying clearly that he'd heard enough from Bertram. It was sinking into the newly blind man how much trouble he was now in. The money to ply his trade had been phenomenal and he got to work on animals that simply didn't come up to work on in any other organisation other than the occasional addition to a museum. From his new sightless vantage, he knew workers compensation insurance wasn't in the agreement he signed and never saw again and had no copy of. Had he thought further he might have been anxious about something more than his eyes.

Kirk dumped the slurry on Jake's face. He realised the man in a strange combination of skins and work clothes hadn't been tied up when Jake lunged at him trying for his throat. Jake was a spent force and there was a reason Chess didn't take Kirk on. Word got around about what Kirk was like when he got angry. And unlike Chess, Kirk was disciplined. Jake soon found a pair or powerful hands around his throat and he was being shaken violently. 'Calm down. You calm down. I want to talk. That's all.' Jake nodded. He was too weak to fight and wanted to find out about Reece. 'Try and get up and come with me to the office. Can we avoid any ridiculous heroics?'

Jake nodded but he could barely stand.

Doc walked in and said. 'I can't find Chess.'

'Shit, is Clive chained up.'

'Yeah.'

He nodded towards Jake. 'Bring him to the office however you can get that done. I've got a call to make.'

Jake was able to lean heavily on the paramedic and take steps putting minimal weight on the injured leg. Kirk got on the radio.

In the gathering gloom Reece had found the second place she needed for her plan. The first being the garage tent. She learned that although they all looked like white tents, some were sitting over modular insulated walls. Others were tents. There were limits to how much the operation could move around when they relocated or packed up for the season and not all places needed insulation. She had pushed the back of a few. At this one she felt only canvas she decided to try to pull it up at the base.

She dug down in the snow behind the tent and found a stake. They were large and driven deep into the frozen ground. She would never be able to pull one up even if she was in good condition and she'd need more than one out to get under the canvas. It was hopeless. She remembered the knife. She thought her chances of cutting the heavy canvas were little better, but she had to try. She found a place right at the back in the middle, down low and plunged the knife as hard as she could. It pierced the canvas which had been used for several seasons so was somewhat perished.

Halfway in it hit a box. The knife had made the tent shiver with the blow. A man came out of the processing room to load up the fire for the evening meal. She moved into the trees, and when he left, she went back and tried to saw the knife up and down to cut the canvas. She learned that if she pulled the cut line out hard it would make the canvas taught enough for the blade to make progress.

She froze when she heard two men talking. She heard a dog she knew was a little restive. She was as still and silent as she could be. A man she didn't know was asking in an irritated tone what the other was doing. She knew the voice of the person answering. He said he and 'Clive' were going to bring her in.

'I'm the one trying to do the damage control Kirk. She can't be far away. Got nowhere to go. But if she dies tonight, we don't know what she knows. There could be people looking for these two and we need to find that out. I'll have her back here in an hour.'

She as relieved at the answer.

Put your gun away and chain Clive up. If you disregard my instructions again Chess, everyone in this camp will be behind you. To run you down. Even the fucking scrawny girl with her magic staff.'

'Go and work in the processing room with Claude. We're short-handed. And get Doc to look at your face.

She had learned that Chess was not in charge, and he was told not to bring her in. She wondered why but was relieved to learn she had a little time until she was certain to be tracked with dogs.

Two doors opened and closed. She cut frantically. A door opened and she heard voices, as a man came out. He walked to the side of the tent she was standing behind to fill a pail it with snow. He was around a corner but only a few feet from where she was standing, exposed.

Once he had left she discovered that she could grip the cut canvas enough so that if she pulled it hard it would tear. The hole was large enough to squeeze into. She knew if she made it too large it would change the way the tension of the canvas sat which would be obvious when anyone entered the tent. She got in and was confronted with the fundamental problem that it was a moonless night, though clear. Starlight was enough for her outside in the snow. But in the tent it was almost completely dark. It had a wooden floor, and she had such a heightened sense of smell she could smell the bottles and cans and jars, many still inside carboard boxes.

Like a dog knowing exactly what's on the dinner table without seeing it, she knew there were condiments and flour and rice and possibly sacks of potatoes. There was also the familiar scent of dried meats and fish, though much higher quality than she and Jake produced. She would be able to follow her nose to get to that. Doors opened and closed. She heard a someone groan in pain. It was Jake. She was relieved.

She could have simply established that this was the stores tent, through the hole and continued to pursue her improbable plan. But her body overrode her. It was screaming for some kind of sustenance. As she felt her way towards the scent of the dried meat she contemplated her situation. Even if she didn't see it to its end, that part of Reece that paid back the daycare children who liked to inflict pain, tease or humiliate was now on fire. In flames about the hope these people had crushed. And now, growing within her, was an anger at what they did. She and Jake had taken so little and marvelled at so much. And they'd been grateful for what they took. These people did the reverse of that.

She was navigating her way around the boxes by feel when she saw a shadow approaching the tent. She was able to get behind a pile of boxes before a man pushed apart the flaps and a light came on.

'Processing. He can get fucked.' This was a voice that she'd heard late that afternoon. The voice which had destroyed a momentary belief that she and Cowboy, against the odds, had made it back to the safety of being with other people. In an instant they knew that for all the dangers they'd confronted, these people would be the worst. She was glad this man had revealed that these people were worse the wolves before they had been trapped by a hot drink.

She was much better at being silent now. This man, for all his unpleasantness had spent years in the wilderness and so was as wary as the wolf Jake has compared him to. He was also a man who mumbled. 'Don't tell me there's no strawberry jam left.' She heard boxes being move and torn open. Piles of boxes unstacked. 'The boss man likes boysenberry, so we all have to eat the shit.' Her sense of smell knew exactly when the lid had been removed of first jam and then peanut butter. There was enough sound to suggest Chess was helping himself to the two condiments using his fingers.

She heard a door to the next building open. 'Is Chess in here? Kirk said he would be. This is ridiculous. I need to get that face of his treated.'

She heard a muffled voice from inside the building. It had a French accent 'He did five minutes work and then fucked off. Five minutes is more than most days, so he'd probably gone to take a rest.' The voice was French Canadian.

'You piece of shit.' Chess hissed as he stalked out of the tent, leaving the light on. There were soon raised voices not far away which gave Reece a chance to get a small armload of dried meat and fish and an uncontaminated jar of jam and peanut butter as the boxes were open with some containers already missing. The raised voices retreated into a room with the door drawn to, however they escalated to shouting. One voice calling for calm, two others finally giving unrestrained vent to grating personalities. One, Claude, saw the devastating events of the afternoon as a good opportunity to point out what he saw as the wide range of Chess's deficiencies.

She looked at the back of the tent before she went to the hole. Although the hole she cut wasn't visible, if one scrutinised that area it would be obvious the canvas wasn't taught. She got out and put the food in the snow and went to the first place she had found.

It was a shed that was open on one side and had spaces for three snowmobiles. But only one was there and it was being worked on with the motor was on a bench. Kirk and everyone else could not deny that Chess was the best of them with mechanics and he'd taken the motor out that afternoon for good reason. She'd risked a moment of lighter flame and saw that the place had everything she needed. On the second visit, something else caught her eye which was worth holding the lighter flame on for. Though for the last two weeks it had been barely lighting. The looming failure of the flint and the gas in the lighter had been another reason that hope in the pair of travellers had been growing thin.

She'd caught sight of a bank of torches and another of lanterns. There must have been twenty in a rack of each all charging from the generator making a quiet hum a hundred meters away in a construction made of earth filled bags and an insulated roof to make it as quiet as possible. It only came on during the peak demand times around mealtimes and long enough to charge a bank of large batteries in a room adjoining the shed. She put her hand over the torch and turned it on long enough to sweep the garage shed to find what she was looking for. The fuel cans. There were four that were full.

A plan that was like running into a pack of wolves had formed in her mind. But she had to have enough energy and warmth to make it work. The fuel cans caused her to add an idea to her plan. She went to the generator shed and saw it was also where the main fuel store was in a large tank with a tap. It was also insulated.

When she came back to get the meat and fish she got two fuel cans from the garage, which she could barely lift, and leaned them against the tent either side of the cut she had made to make it taut again.

Once she'd seen all these things needed she was running in the starlight. Chess's dog slept irrespective of what went on in camp. He wasn't a watch dog. However, on the far side of the camp she heard other dogs. They didn't sound friendly. However she believed she had to take the risk going around to recover Boo Boo as it was not too far out of way her way to where she wanted to start her plan. It was partly to warm herself up and also to have the familiar scent and comfort it had supplied for so long, When she arrived she was shocked to see that the man who Jake had killed was still there. It led her to believe the people she was dealing with must be utterly ruthless. She would need to be the same. In the starlight she saw he had something on his belt she was glad to relieve him of.

The plan was taking on greater dimensions. She put a boot covered in slimy fur on the big man's face and pulled out the pike.

While she had been in the tent, she heard Doc leave the barracks with Jake. Kirk was on the radio. An activity they endeavoured to keep to a minimum even though it was a bespoke band width and only a local area signal.

'Return to base.' This had been the most disastrous day in his working life, so he hoped he was able to convey the need for them to comply purely by the tone of his voice.

'A shame. The fishing's good up here. Found a good place we were going to try out tomorrow.' They were on the trail of something special.

'I'll say it again. Return to base.'

At that moment the door opened as Doc tried to navigate Jake into the room. Kirk turned, as he had done three times that day, to his cost, he waved them off.

Jake heard. 'Right now?' The voice coming over the airwaves was annoyed.

'No. Not now. Is it not dark where you are? Christ. In the morning.'

Jake heard this as the door closed. They both waited outside saying nothing. To Doc, Jake was the man who killed Davey. To Jake, Doc was a part of a group of people that would neither welcome them, nor let them go. They stood in silence for five minutes until Kirk came out and, annoyed as if Doc should have known the call was finished; said 'Well come on.'

Doc helped Jake to a chair. It was an office with a desk and two chairs. No one knew who the other chair was for because Kirk welcomed no one to sit in his office. Until tonight.

Doc was dismissed with a nod.

Kirk became strangely relaxed which Jake found odd considering he had killed one of his men and Reece had badly injured two others. It was partly because Kirk didn't have a relationship with any of his employees in which he could be candid and have a drink. He also knew being tense or aggressive in this meeting would not serve his ends.

He pulled out the bottle from a location not so much hidden, simply out of view. It was a 'dry camp' which Chess ignored but it was the one thing he was successfully discreet about. Kirk had a bottle of scotch.

It was sometimes untouched for weeks and when it was, it was usually about a milestone achieved or some very special trophy they'd been able to acquire. Though more recently when he'd needed a 'Chess De-stress' from time to time.

'I'm Kirk. Drink?'

'No. Thankyou.' Jake didn't intend to make the interview an easy one. He knew how things would end irrespective of what was said. He'd regained consciousness soon after he'd been put in the room with the blind taxidermist and so had heard how Kirk spoke to him. Jake foolishly thought he might overpower someone when they were expecting him to be disoriented.

'Must be quite a story. You're a long way from anywhere wearing the skins of at least six kinds of animals I can count. Haven't been eating a great deal, if I can put it that way.'

'Plane crash.'

'I hadn't heard of one. Anywhere in Canada. I keep abreast of such things.'

'It's what's happened.'

'I would guess it's been a long time since you've had a coffee or a hot chocolate maybe. Could I exchange one for you, introduce yourself and your travelling companion.'

Jake could see no harm in it and the very concept of a hot chocolate sent his mind into a paroxysm of desire. 'I'm Jake and my friend is Reece.'

Kirk put on a kettle and prepared the makings of a hot chocolate. 'How long have you been walking.'

'Late summer.'

They said nothing more until Jake had spent some time with his hot chocolate and Kirk with his scotch. Then the boss of the camp said. 'We need to come to some arrangement about how you…leave here.'

'Yeah about that. I have a good idea what you people do. I've got a reasonable gauge on your level of concern about the man I killed, and the one badly hurt who was lying in the room with me.'

'You were awake.'

'I should have pretended to wake up. Didn't realise I was going to get slush thrown on me. I could have done without that.'

Kirk came to the point. 'Would a promise to give you supplies and to take you as far south as our own fuel needs permit on a snow mobile be of interest.'

'If it was true.'

Kirk smiled and nodded. 'Good...Jake. Let's not waste time. How about a promise that I can be held to. You can stare right into my eyes and I think you'll believe me. You convince your friend...Reece wasn't it...that we are going to give you those supplies and take you out to move on. Then you both can have a pleasant meal and I'll take you out on one of our machines and it will be quick and painless. I have men here who need to at least see you leave alive and with provisions. They need to hear that's what you want. Hear that you don't want us to call the authorities partly because of what you did this afternoon, but also, I'll have it put about; that there are some other issues which is why you're out here in the first place. Now even if some or all my men know that it's all theatre, they all observed the same piece of theatre and can come to any other conclusions they want.'

Jake said nothing.

'That's one promise. The other is, if you create trouble for me, make accusations, ask for help from my men, try to escape...whatever. I will make it very very unpleasant for you and I won't care who sees it.' His voice took on a trace of nastiness which Jake could see was not foreign to him. 'You have destroyed this operation for this season and in this region.'

'I don't have the manpower, the skills and I have a liability of dead and injured to manage. I have decided not to direct my anger at you and your friend because I think we have both had the misfortune in encountering the same person.'

Jake didn't flinch at his gaze. 'Reece would never believe the first story because she's smarter than I am and will have figured out our hope of being helped in any way by your…organisation the same as I did. She'll have more respect if she gets told the real story up front.'

'And will she accept it.'

Jake was reflective. 'I don't like the idea of making you feel any better about this. We knew we had…a couple nights at most. We wouldn't have got through even one if a blizzard came along. Our only hope was to get to some outpost of civilisation. Which this turned out not to be.'

Kirk ignored the slight. 'Very Well. You and I take Clive, I'll enjoy taking that idiot's dog whether he likes it or not, and we'll find her. Have a conversation. You both come back here. Don't mingle. Having committed murder and assault that shouldn't be too difficult. Have a nice meal. Fill some of our packs up from the provisions tent, and I drive you out.'

'A long way out of earshot where I know there are a few bears in springtime. Not big enough to be of interest to us. I don't want any remains. Only a story. Mainly to tell the people I work for. I know this is the only story they will want to hear should they ever need to remember one.'

'Yeah.' Said Jake quietly. 'She might have died of exposure by the time we find her.'

'I can work with that. You would decide you want me to take her remains a long way from here and you'll go the way she went.'

They were quiet for a long time. Jake could have gulped his hot chocolate but had savoured it instead. He said something, not specifically for Kirk to hear, but because he wanted to say it and he wanted someone to hear it. 'We really believed we could make it. We came so close to dying, in the first hours after the crash. Came so close to dying many times but we worked hard, had some luck and kept going.' He finished quietly. 'That girl.' His eyes were welling up. 'She killed a fully grown caribou with a stick I carved. We took on wolf packs. We believed…'

It cost Kirk nothing to be honest. 'I'm not pleased at how things must happen, but I'm not flexible either.'

'Seems to me you're off the land and Reece must be tough and I believe you when you say…intelligent.' He breathed out heavily. 'To be honest, I would prefer each of you was taking a space on the roster I have. I didn't choose the man you know spoke to and I can see now some of the men I did choose weren't the best picks I've made. We crossed paths in the wrong circumstances Jake.'

'Yeah.' Jake would have thought this was simply a means for Kirk to make himself feel better by handing out a few compliments and an alternative reality. However from what he'd seen Kirk was all pragmatism and no sentiment. He was expressing a frank opinion. How he could imagine that either he or Reece would ever participate in what they were doing showed Jake that Kirk had gaps in his understanding of people. He was hiring people, the values of whom he could not fully assess.

'Okay. Some pain killers for you, stitches and a hot meal perhaps.' This was Kirk at his most hospitable. Jake saw no point in being disagreeable even if Kirk was going to kill them. They had no options and if he tried to plead his case with his men it would likely unleash a side to Kirk he kept a rein on. He also hoped that if he was complaint, he would not get tied up. Be ready for anything.

Chess and Claude had finished their argument, violence avoided through the interventions of Doc, initially with reasonableness. Ultimately with a threat to go and get Kirk. All of this had driven Davey from their minds.

Kirk helped Jake to the door and left him outside. No one was ever in his office alone. He found the three men in the processing room and knew there had been some kind of altercation. He was losing interest in these people rapidly. He directed Doc to 'stitch that man up' and for Claude to get the evening meal ready. To Chess. 'Get back to work.' He turned and left. There had been so much going on he needed to stop, have a scotch, and process it all. That's what he was good at. He needed to craft a communication to the people who ran the operation. He had intended to let the man who paid for the operation know what had befallen his investment sooner rather than later. But now he had changed his mind. Kirk had other plans to make.

A slow cooked stew was ready. Claude was the camp cook as well as a specialist on hides and skins, which were taken off where the animal was killed. The animals head or antlers as were brought in depending on whether it met the criteria. Chess took his turn out in the field as a shooter but was not the preferred partner of either of the two men who did most of the hunting and went alone with Clive.

He spent quite a bit of his time out scoping areas and brought in a worthwhile quantity of skins and trophy heads on his own. It was a feature of their dislike for Chess that they attributed the success to Clive. Flawed as Chess might be, he had lived in the wilderness since his earliest memories. He was an excellent shot and a good judge of what to take. With his variety of competencies and his dog, Chess would have been a highly valued member of the team if he wasn't a native-born asshole.

Kirk came into the barracks as the medic finished what was a simple stitching procedure. Doc said nothing to Jake while he did this. Jake knew Doc was an example of a person whose values didn't match his workplace. He also knew the paramedic didn't comprehend the inevitable fate Jake and Reece were destined for which had taken Jake seconds to apprehend. 'Have you treated Chess's face yet.'

'Not yet. Kirk I'm not going to…' Kirk was surprised Doc was going to repeat what he'd suggested regarding the treatment of Chess's face in the hearing of Jake and Bertram. This all confirmed he needed to clean house.

'Yes. I know what you're going to do. Treat his wounds now. Unless you decide to leave them untreated Doc. He's in the processing room.'

'We'll be having a group meeting after the meal and people will need to get plenty of rest tonight as we may break camp tomorrow.'

'How are we going to get…'

'Do as I've asked.'

Doc was tired. 'A please costs nothing Kirk. Maybe things would run more smoothly if you treated people like there weren't dogshit.'

Kirk was well past caring what any of these people thought. 'Doc would you go and give me an example of your work so I can express my gratitude for it. Please.'

The meal was ready. Claude wasn't going to make the bread rolls he was known for. His companions didn't realise what a blow it was for him to lose Davey and in such a violent way. He realised in that moment they hadn't even gone to recover his friends body. He could not help but take some of the blame. But like everyone he been drawn into Chess's shit, but he also didn't want to be involved in bringing him in and was unsure where Kirk was going to put his remains in the camp. He went to talk to Doc about it, but he found him with Chess in the processing room and quickly retreated.

Doc had arrived to find a man balling and unballing his fists. It was what his mother had taught him when he was a boy when she was at her wits end trying to manage his anger. 'Calm yourself Chess'. Doc thought it strange that he hadn't sought out treatment yet with puncture wounds to his face and a torn ear. Maybe Chess saw it was a sign of weakness. Doc didn't care. He realised he didn't like anyone he worked with other than Davey who was dead and Bertram who was heading that way. The idea of winding up the season was attractive now, irrespective of the amount of money he would lose. But he knew things about the operation. And he would lean on them if he believed he was short changed. Doc saw a man making what efforts he was capable of. 'Come on Chess, let's get you fixed up eh?'

Kirk went into the barracks and spoke to Jake. 'Can you walk?' Jake knew Kirk was saying he should crawl if he needed to. 'Go and sit by the fire.'

Kirk needed to see Bertram. And once Jake had staggered out said. 'Is the pain being managed well enough.'

'Doc says he's pumped in anything they would have in a hospital, and a bit more. It's not too bad, I know it's wearing off though and I'll need another shot soon.'

'You want a hot drink. I know you can't sit up and drink it, but I have a cup with a bent straw that might work. Coffee. Hot Chocolate. Though now that I think of it you're a tea drinker.'

'Yeah, my parents were from Britain and that's where I went to study.'

Kirk got instruction on how he liked it and brought it to him and held it while Bertram drew small amounts through the straw. It had not been made with boiling water, which was essential, he had been taught, to release the flavour or the tea. But at least it was something warm and sweet.

'This is my ninth season Bertram. Between here and other places we work in the world. I've seen my share of taxidermists. Some good. Some less so. You're the best I've seen. I've booked a call with the Owner of the operation. I'm going to tell him that tomorrow or the next day at the absolute latest we need to get you out of here. We can probably get a Twin Otter with skis to land not too far away. It took me some time to get my head straightened out. What's gone on here has been...I don't know what to say. You understand it's taken me some time to get my priorities right.'

'Hey Kirk. I was worried yeah. But it was for a few hours and now…I've got some…confidence I know I'm going to get out of here soon.' His voice broke a little. Treatment was one thing. Facing the rest of his life was another.

Bertram had finished most of the tea and Kirk's mind moved to other things. 'There will be a group meeting this evening. We'll be breaking camp as soon as we've got you on a plane. I'll come and check on you later.'

The pain relief drugs were acting as a sedative. Bertram's mind had now become preoccupied with his future. He needn't have worried. He would be unconscious soon and dead in a few hours. Kirk had given him something he'd used on two other occasions when someone inconvenient needed to die in their sleep.

The kitchen doubled as a mess with a table which could take six. It was used when the weather was bad. If it was a pleasant evening, they had the meal around the fire. Kirk usually took his meal in his office.

The mood was strange. Two of the team were not in their usual places. Two had shed any pretence and openly despised each other. Doc had reflected on what Kirk had asked him to do to Chess and his lack of concern for Betram and was angry.

All Chess had wanted was a bandage to the ear and some disinfectant. He did however demand pain killers. About which he knew a great deal. Doc was wrong to think he left his wounds exposed due to manliness. He planned to get to her first. And she would get a good look at his face. Kirk and the other 'fucking suburbanites' could do what they wanted. She was going to get that antler staff driven into her face. Twice. Then he'd take his dog and a gun. Six hundred miles didn't matter to him in any season. He already had a pack behind the barracks full of everything he needed. Including half the drugs in the place.

Jake, who had killed one of their group not three hours before, sat to the side, trying not to bolt his stew. He knew Reece better than anyone ever had. Be ready for anything.

Kirk was reflecting on what to do next. Or rather how to do it. He needed to get one thing done first. It was time to go and find the girl and come back to say the pair decided to run rather than face the consequences for what they'd done. He'd agreed to this, and he was going to take them one rucksack full of food. Kirk wouldn't use a gun. Jake would get the knife first from someone who'd been slaughtering, skinning and butchering animals since before Chess was born.

The remains of his team would be told to begin to pack up the camp while he was gone, which was no small exercise. He'd call a small gathering by Bertram's bedside, who would have been found dead, before the two in the field arrived back. Only a moment of their attention on someone everyone had liked. Maybe share a story about how Bertram would get excited about what Chess brought in and tell him how he was going to do 'amazing things' with them. Kirk would have his handgun. Chess first. Not because he disliked him. It would be because he was unquestionably the most dangerous. The others would give him that moment of surprise which was all he needed. Doc next. Then Claude. The two from the field would be killed with a hunter's rifle. From three hundred yards as they rode in.

The boss was going to have to line up what would likely be a Twin Otter ski plane to get the merchandise out of there in a few trips. They had nearly half of their quota. Some very rare pieces. He was starting to think it was time to change employer. These weren't the only people in town looking for someone with his skill set and appetite for risk. And he didn't plan on giving the boss the full inventory. He never did. There was always one or two skins, maybe a trophy if he could manage it.

The bonus he got was, he believed, less than he deserved. This time he could take tenfold in merchandise with a few choice hides.

There was no conversation. A group of men were sitting around a fire. Each displeased about their situation. It was almost time for Kirk to suggest that he, Jake and Clive would be bringing the girl in. 'I know what you want.' They heard a clear voice. It was a long way away but carried in the still cold air.

They all looked up. The dogs that were chained up growled. And Clive, who took his meal at Chess's feet was immediately alert.

'If you let Jake go and give us some food, I'll come over there for the night. Then we both leave.'

Chess snorted at the stupidity of the girl.

'You be quiet.' Kirk hissed. In a voice also clear and projected to reach the significant distance the girl had chosen to speak from he said. 'Reece. You have...been given the wrong impression about this operation. This is a business, and I am the manager. I'm Kirk. We are a legitimate, licenced operation. I can show you the paperwork. Your friend Jake has seen it all.'

Reece said nothing. From listening to them, she already knew that most of these men would not tolerate the misuse a sixteen-year-old. And probably not even Chess. However, she was equally sure they would not take them back to civilisation. She'd been shocked to find the body of the man Jake had killed laying where he fell, pike still stuck through the back of his head, gradually freezing in the cold air. It had been to her advantage though, and Davey was left in an even worse condition when she left him.

She had needed something to cause a distraction to fulfil a later part of her plan. So she had gone back to where Davey lay as the men were called to dinner. He was a big man. Thighs bigger than Boo Boo's. She had a sharp knife now and so worked quickly. She cut though his trousers well below the groin and sliced off a large slab of flesh from each inner thigh. They were not quite frozen; however the blood was crystalized and not flowing. She'd cut up a lot of meat and she was doing this in the starlight. So she treated the task like she had with Boo Boo. It was tiring and she needed to cut his shirt off also. She would need it. It was a part of the plan. When she was nearly through the second portion of Davey's thigh, she heard a growl from behind her. She was grateful. The wolf could have simply loped in and attacked.

She dropped the knife and picked up her antler clad staff which was right below her hand and swung it around. The three wolved moved back. They'd seen that before. They'd been following the tracks of the two humans moving more and more slowly. However in their last encounter they'd paid a bitter price, and they got a sense this particular human wasn't afraid. In fact she was pleased they'd arrived. Taking on the two dogs which were chained up had been a major anxiety. The wolves kept their distance; snarling. She picked up the pieces of Davey she'd cut, wrapped them in his shirt took his knife and her staff and backed away. Walking back she realised cutting up a person had helped to tip her over. She had driven her spear into two people's faces to defend herself and her friend. Now she was ready to attack again. These people were going to kill her and Jake. She had no doubt. They were worse than wolves who would kill to eat. These men would kill to cover up an activity she found repugnant. She felt sorry for the wolves they'd killed. Two out of the pack. She would be delighted if she could get even two of these human wolves.

The girl going to high school six months before may not have had such a strong reaction when learning of such an operation.

The Reece of that night had lived among these animals. Struggled among them. If things died there should be a reason. And it should be about that struggle.

She'd listened to a few conversations and tried to assess what the personalities she attributed to them would do. In what she thought the two most likely scenario's dogs would be involved. She thought there were four or five men in the camp plus Jake whom she assumed would be tied up or worse. She could never hope to confront so many, so she had a plan in six parts. It had started as a very basic idea but had grown as her mind caught fire with spite and menace A mind that knew she would never out power power. But was determined to try to outsmart it one risky step at a time until she was caught.

Kirk had to think quickly in composing an answer for Reece She wasn't going to be convinced she and Jake could fill some backpacks and walk out of there. 'Keep quiet.' He said this so he could exchange a glance with each member of the party who were all looking at him. His glance said. Humour me. However, Chess was not able to grasp subtlety.

'Reece. Your friend Jake has told me a little about you. Taking on wolves. Spearing a Caribou.' Jake wasn't sure he liked these details being repeated by someone like Kirk.

He thought it may not have been wise to share them. 'From what I've heard, I'm certain we could get to like each other Reece.' Those sitting around the fire found that an unlikely statement. 'Ironically we find ourselves shorthanded now. We're only halfway through the season.' They carried out these activities because there was less scrutiny in winter, albeit it was harder to acquire some animals though these orders were usually filled in early spring. Some animals were easier to find in winter because they stayed in one place.

'We have a lot of work with hides and looking after the camp but also trips out into the wilderness. I've spoken with Jake about it, and you can hear from him what he thinks.' He gave Jake a look which made it clear things would be unpleasant for both of them if he wasn't convincing.

Be ready for anything. He would give her any chance he could. He knew if these men paid a price, they would both die happier if they could even land a blow on these people. They shared far more similarities than differences. He spoke out clearly. 'Reece. You and me both know we were finished. Had a few nights left in us. That's without bad weather. We both accepted that. Things… things got off to a bad start here. There's a way forward though. Reece…honey…' Jake would never, ever call her that. 'I know you don't really want to live with your dad anymore.

And school, it's pointless for you the way you're treated.' Reece's relationship with most of the people at school figured as much in her life as her relationship with her parents. Barely relevant and temporary. Though she had a group of friends and teachers she valued. Jake knew that. His voice was flavoured with one making more than purely a suggestion. 'So maybe we give this a try. Hell, I can't deny I'd love to do some hunting…if I…get like promoted up to that.' His voice was submissive at the end of that sentence as one who might have been a little presumptuous in front of the boss. 'And from what I've been told we'd even get paid. Anyhow…I think maybe it's the best plan. You should…think about it.'

Jake had told her everything she needed to know. She had thought there might be a slight possibility she would execute her plan and inflict whatever damage she could on a group not intent on killing them.

No one said anything. Kirk waited for her to speak. Chess sighed theatrically. Her voice came back clear but uncertain. 'This is…this isn't what I was expecting. I can't see how…after what I did.'

'Reece, we can manage that. Accidents happen out in the wilderness. Wild animals. A fall. There's no upside to anyone in blaming people for what happened.'

'I have a plan to get Bertram the professional treatment he needs very soon. Like I say. You might get to like working together with us and there could be work here every season if, as Jake says, school isn't…enough for you. And it's good money.'

'I…I've got to think about this…'

Kirk wanted to get the situation contained. The story would be that on balance, they would decide they'd prefer to leave with provisions. He could not keep the annoyance from creeping into his voice. 'Reece. There aren't a lot of options for you. We have a fire, hot food, a soft warm bed. And Jake's here. Ready to stay with us like he says.'

Reece pretended to be an irritated, petulant and slightly sullen teenager. 'I know that. Do you think I didn't hear him. Do you think I'm stupid. This has been really hard for me. I'm only young you know. And Jake already bosses me around most of the time and now I'll have a whole bunch of people doing that. I know I'll only be a shit kicker and yeah that's probably the best I can hope for. But you can imagine that I'm not thrilled about the idea.'

'Reece that's not what I said. We have important work for you here.'

Jake leaned across. Like he was a little embarrassed to have given her such fulsome praise earlier. 'You can see why she has a bit of trouble in school.'

Kirk didn't give a flying fuck about any of this. Though it was going to make it easier to dispatch her if she was a whining brat. Curiously, Jake would be harder than the others.

Reece was whining now. 'Give me some time. Okay. I know what you said. I was real worried at the way that man was talking when we first met. I need…I fucking…I want some time alone. Can you people leave me alone for a while. I'll…come in soon…I left something out in the woods. I didn't want anyone to take it. It's my Boo Boo. I'll be back soon.'

Chess was shaking his head. 'Her fucking Boo Boo.' He reached down and touched Clive and said a word. It was an Innuit word. Chess was not very good with people. However he was exceptional with dogs. Dogs didn't bring out the undesirable traits his two legged counterparts did in Chess. He'd told Clive to hold the target until he arrived.

The dog shot into the night.

'What the fuck are you doing call that dog back now.' Kirk kept his voice down.

'Kirk you think the Old Man hates me. Guess what. Maybe it suits him that you believe that. Maybe I get on with him better than you realise, and he tells me I'm here partly to keep an eye on you and report back. I've never done that because that's not the kind of man I am. But now. This. We got one man killed and two been mutilated and you're going to give these fuckers a job. Are you kidding me?' Everyone else around the fire knew Kirk would say anything it took to bring the girl in voluntarily if he could. What happened after that no one knew. However, Doc and Claude knew it would have to be acceptable to them. They'd been pushed far enough, and no amount of money was going to make them become the men they had never dreamed of being.

Chess stood up. 'I'll bring her into the camp. She can have that hot meal and that warm bed. But she and her friend can also tell us the full story of how they came to be here and who else knows about it. Then we might call the Old Man before we start the job interviews. Jesus.' He walked off and then had to walk back to get a torch. He had a plan. And it didn't involve bringing her back in.

'Claude go with him and...'

Kirk knew Clive would be holding her wherever she was. Even if he was sitting patiently at the base of a tree.

'No. Fuck you Claude. I don't want to listen to any more of your bullshit. I don't need some fucking Kanuk in my ear.' Kirk did not realise Chess might have the kind of strategic anger he would measure out when it suited his purposes.

By this time Clive was dead. Reece had put some pieces of cut up Davey meat in the pathway of the dogs she believed would come at her so that they might pause while she struck, though she suspected they wouldn't be distracted by it. Indeed, it meant nothing to Clive, he had a few tasks. He held what had been injured and was at risk of getting away and dying pointlessly in the forest. And he was exceptional at tracking game even if it had passed by before a snowfall. Silently, giving Chess a sign when they were well back and so not giving it any clue to the game he and Chess approached. Chess was the most skilled hunter in the camp. Clive only knew Chess as someone who showed him respect and affection. Chess's father trained his dogs that way. Which was ironic, because he didn't treat people that way.

Least of all his biological son. Who had escaped drunken abuse with his sister and mother; a child bride in a backwoods cabin after she'd beaten him senseless with a cast iron pan and they had run for days through the woods. Twelve years later she had reinvented herself and remarried in the city.

Chess, in his early teens, had stayed with his mother and away from the wilderness for only two years. He migrated back to the man with whom he had a complex relationship. He hated his father but that didn't mean he didn't respect him as a hunter and dog trainer. The boy navigated the episodes of drunken violence, exacerbated by the escape of his mother, and came and went from the family cabin. Working occasionally on the fringes of civilisation and bringing supplies in for his father. Sometimes liquor that Chess learned they could share with a species of fellowship for a few hours before the son would disappear for a week or a month. When they were both sober, he learned a great deal from a man who he never saw bettered in the wilderness.

Vanessa, his sister and now the Old Man's stepdaughter, was more the strategist and opportunist like her mother. She'd suggested her mother's second and wealthy husband be introduced to the wonders of the wilderness. His response to this was to despoil it. The stepson eventually developed an uneasy relationship with the 'other' father. The Old Man was not entirely enthusiastic about it. However it was Chess, on trips from pontoon and ski planes into areas never visited, that revealed the true potential these areas could offer.

He absorbed enough of the romance of the landscape, guns, dogs and hunters to share stories in smoke filled studies or with Emirs in their six-star hotel rooms. On his most recent trip a few years earlier now, the Old Man had even met Clive who barely needed the embellishments that stories of him were prone to. Clive brought out the best in Chess. And irrespective of Kirk's assumption that anyone could work with the dog, Chess, excelling at only one kind of relationship, brought out the best in Clive.

Clive had never been sent to work at night or to hold a human. There was no point to the former, and it was dangerous. The dog had an exceptional sense of smell but was equally good at homing in a sound. And that was the touch and word Chess gave the dog. Go and hold what you heard. However, the animal had left a floodlit compound into a moonless night and had only moments to establish night vision. He was slowing as he approached her. He would circle around his prey to find a place to hold it. It had never been a person though. The starlight provided a surprising amount of light reflected from the snow for Reece having been acclimatised to it for over an hour. She ran forward as she expected the dog or dogs to slow. She was relieved to see only one. She lifted the pike, lunging it forward. She couldn't risk breaking her antler staff.

She needed it. There was only one chance with the pike, though the short stabbing sticks were in her belt and she planned to be viscous to fend off an attack. She hoped for the pike to hit it in the forehead, ideally catch it in an eye socket. All she wanted was to cause it to be hurt and surprised enough to run or at least be weakened in its attack, though that would give the next part of the plan away. Clive didn't bark and rarely growled. However, he had his mouth open enough, ready to take hold of her. That allowed the pike, above and beyond her intentions, to be driven in by a combination of his momentum and her lunge.

The dog, admired by all who knew it, didn't make a sound. It writhed briefly and died. The pike driven through its entire body. There was an immediate feeling of equal parts relief and regret. She cared nothing for the owner. She regretted the two wolves they'd killed, probably a third or even fourth dying after the altercation. This was a dog approaching without the slightest aggression irrespective of appearances. Her flames of anger were building. They'd put her in this position. To defend herself by killing a dog she'd heard enough in the conversation around the camp to know it was one of the best examples of the species. She had moved forward half a dozen paces from where she wanted Clive to be positioned.

So she dragged him to exactly where she needed him and waited, hoping there wasn't more than two people. It had been tiring dragging a dog on a pike a few yards. She wasn't sure she could even handle one person but two was the most likely scenario. She had some ideas for two, but her chances would be slim. Her staff waited leaning against the tree below her. She hoped the hunters would have torches.

Soon she was confronted with another person with limited night vision. They were supposed to find a pike and some lumps of meat next to a shirt which they might decide to look more closely at. But the man with the torch immediately ran to the dog. He was disbelieving at first and then a rage started to build. This person. This scrawny fucking kid had come in and turned his life upside down in the space of hours. He stood up. He was going to get the other dogs and his gun and she would find out what no one else had ever really seen even if they thought they had. She would see how nasty he could be. But a weight landed on him from a tree above. He'd been standing a little further out than would have been ideal, but she pushed off and led the fall with Davey's knife.

She was scrawny and it plunged in with less force and accuracy than she'd hoped into his shoulder rather than his neck and was turned sideways by the scapula.

As she had done with her antler staff she knew she had to strike quickly and as many times as possible. Chess had good reflexes. His father had been a mean drunk, so he'd learned to move quickly in response to the violent or unexpected however he was looking down at the personality in his life he loved most. Dead. Reece got one more strike in on the crest of his shoulder, but it angled away from his neck again and slid in above his collar bone and came out below it. He shrugged at the same time as he reached up to take a hold of any part of her he could grasp. She had spent time thinking about how to approach the attack and where she wanted to land so she pushed backwards with her knees and, reluctantly leaving the knife, used its handle to push Chess forward and herself back. He staggered. It allowed her time to scurry around the tree she had leapt from and recover her Shaft. Sut not run. Chess stumbled but didn't fall and was left groping for the knife to pull it out. However he so enraged he decided not to waste the precious seconds he might lose in catching her and driving the antler staff if he could find it into her as many places as he needed to 'Calm the Rage' then take the pike out of Clive and skewer her with it. And he wasn't going to run anymore. Kirk was going to pay. No one had inflicted such damage upon him. And this on a person, man and boy; who had been brutally beaten on more than one occasion.

And she had stolen the one thing that he loved most in the world. They could have taken her in the daylight with no problem. The girl, her friend, Kirk and that fucking Kanuck were all going to pay.

He swung the flashlight around and saw part of the antler staff exposed behind the trees she was hiding behind. However Reece wasn't hiding. She was waiting. He pointed the light right where her eyes should have been and came around the tree as swiftly as he possibly could as soon as he saw it. The staff was withdrawn and brought down and low. She lunged up and pushed it in front of her from the crouching position she'd been waiting in and drove the staff at the light smashing the glass and tearing into Chess's fingers and palms. With the light out they were both temporarily blinded, and it was time to run and, she hoped, capitalise on Chess's return to the camp and the attention that would draw. She was going to chance the next part of her plan whatever the case. Chess had kept quiet to this point because he wanted to have the time with her before anyone else arrived. Now he realised she'd laid a trap which he had been completely taken in by.

Chess could cope with pain. He drew the knife out and covered the area of the second stab wound with only his hand initially, kneeled briefly and stoked Clive as his eyes adjusted, and shoved the knife in his belt. He would use it later. He wasn't going to return to the camp. He'd get his gun next to his pack and take the dogs.

However Claude approached with a light and asked what was happening. Claude had taken his time getting a torch, which most of the people in the camp always carried, and indeed Claude already had one, but had concealed it. He didn't want to confront Chess alone hence he spoke loudly from a distance, ready to run. Kirk had stood and was about to go to his office to get something he also wouldn't reveal. The camp boss had begun to suspect what Chess was intending. For the girl, and possibly all of them. His response would be justifiable. Saving an 'innocent' girl even if she did die of her wounds later. The French Canadian had been moving slowly. He shone the light in Chess's eyes as if it was necessary to identify him which robbed Chess of what night vision he'd developed. It was a pettiness which Claude would take any opportunity to invent from now on to retaliate for all Chess had said, done and not done. The fabric of what had been an uneasy collaboration in the operation was in shreds.

'Get that fuck_ng light out my eyes you Kanuck prick, or I'll ram it down your fucking throat.'

'Where's Clive?' Claude almost shouted this. It alerted all in the camp of Chess's whereabouts.

Chess pushed past him roughly. Realising too late it would cause a stabbing pain to his own shoulder. Claude having called and now following him with a light meant he could hardly push through with his plan. Unless he wanted to get his gun and hold it on Kirk he would need to wait. She would keep. He walked well away from the fire towards where a first aid kit was bolted to the barracks hut to get some padding bandages. He would need Doc's help and intended to call Doc to where he waited.

Kirk, diverted from getting the pistol that as better concealed than the scotch. He appeared right in front of Chess. 'What the fuck just happened.'

'I need to see Doc for a minute.'

'Doc said. 'Sure.' Seeing the whole of Chess's shoulder drenched in blood. He wished he hadn't allowed them to give him that nickname.

'Come over to the fire if you want to see him. And call Clive in.' Kirk turned away and walked back to the fire tossing Doc a look that he should go back to where he'd been sitting.

Chess didn't have better options. He needed to get to his gun. He knew as well as anyone Kirk had been killing animals with a knife for a lifetime. Indeed at the beginning of every season in every location he made the first 'kills' and gave everyone a 'demonstration' as to what he expected in terms of dispatching, skinning, taking trophies and taking meat. He did this even if there were no changes to the team from one season to the next. Chess could feel his shirt saturating with blood and the hand that had carried the torch was punctured in two places in the palm plus the thumb pad torn. The drugs Doc had given him, in addition to those he had liberated from the store before surrendering to an urge for peanut butter and jam.

Doc was going to ignore Kirk and get what he needed to treat the wounds when Kirk said 'Wait.' It was a voice that carried absolute authority and an overt threat. He drew up a chair near where he sat and bade Chess to sit. 'What...the fuck...just happened.'

Chess looked sideways to avoid Kirk's eyes, composed a sour face and said. 'Clive's dead. Then the fucking bitch snuck up and stabbed me in the back.'

Kirk glanced at Chess's hand, bleeding profusely now. Doc started to say he needed to get to work on Chess, but Kirk held up his hand. 'And.'

'I turned around with the light and she pushed that fucking antler thing at me and it took the light out.'

The silence was broken by a sound in the distance that caused the camp dogs to growl and bark occasionally on their chains. The sound was something that made Kirk even more unhappy. But he would deal with one source of unhappiness at a time. He knew he should be reacting to what had happened, not dissecting it. However he'd had enough of this useless destructive asshole, and he was going to drag every detail out in front of an audience even though he didn't give a fuck about them and they would soon all be dead. 'Quite an attacker. Kills Clive. Who was smarter than you by quite a margin. The scrawny starving kid then nails you with a knife with one hand, on the top of your shoulder and then once she's finished doing that she's also carrying this crazy spear in the other hand and she nails you again.'

Chess said nothing.

'Is there anything you believe you can contribute of value to this operation that would suggest to me I shouldn't let you bleed to death. Except of course for the fact that you're going to call my boss and explain to him that you're the ideas man. You're the decisive one that goes and gets things fixed. You're his eyes and ears. Have I got all that right.'

'I'll sit here and bleed to death if that's what you're angling for Kirk. I'm not going to beg for anything from a man like you.'

Doc interrupted. 'Okay Chess. Let's get you looked after.' Kirk held up his hand and gave Doc a look some people had not lived long to remember.

During this conversation Reece was moving as quietly as she could in the stores tent. She brought in the two twenty litre fuel cans that were leaning against the canvas near the cut line and holding it tight. She began quietly pouring one over all the boxes at the back and opened the lid on the other can and dribbling some in a line and spilled some out of it on the boxes as near the front as she dared and left the second can open leaning next to the wet cardboard. She was listening intently to the conversation. Chess was reluctantly recounting what happened. She had a feeling she would need more fuel to get the result she wanted.

Based on the conversation, she risked a trip to the garage shed to bring back another can leaving the last one there for the next phase. The dogs chained at the far side of the compound were focused on the sounds coming from the opposite direction to her. If she got this phase to work she had a circuit to run to make the playing field as close to level as she could get it. Once she had the provisions tent set up there was a twinge of reluctance to see this happen to the stores. She also knew in the still air if she tried to light anything up while in the tent, she would go up with it. She had planned to light up a fuel-soaked rag and throw it in the slit she'd made and hope the canvas protected her from the initial flash.

It was at this point. After being so faithful for so long, the lighter fluid ran out. It had been showing the signs of having little left to give for some time. She kept clicking it and clicking it.

Nothing. She could hear Kirk talking however she got a sense he wasn't usually someone who talked in long monologues. Though on this occasion, useful or not, he could not help but fully explore and expose what he saw as the depth of Chess's unmitigated stupidity.

She went back into the tent, almost gagging on the fumes that would result in nothing without a flame. She had her hand almost completely covering the torch. Hoping they stored something she could use in the tent.

Having completed the process of castigating Chess, she heard Kirk say in a voice encompassing the assembled group. 'Okay. Moving on. Can someone tell me why I hear wolves around our camp. We kill wolves. It's a part of our business. And then we skin them.'

Chess was very sour now. 'I imagine they followed those two walking carcasses you wanted to make employees of.'

'Those wolves are fighting over something.'

'It's probably Davey.' Said Claude quietly. Reluctantly; guilty and sad. 'I remembered while I was making dinner and then you said there was a meeting and I…' The truth was Claude couldn't face it. He and Davey had been closer than they dared to let anyone know. Least of all Chess and Kirk. He was going to talk to Doc, but Kirk took his meal with them which he didn't often do. Then the girl who'd put Bertram's eyes out had called to them while the man who'd killed Davey sat eating the stew Claude had cooked not a dozen paces from where he sat.

Kirk spun around. 'Davey?'

'Yeah.' Doc didn't care what Kirk thought and was only too happy to get out in front of Claude, who between his skirmishing with Chess and the death of Davey was disintegrating. 'There have been…distractions.'

'Distractions. You leave one of our fucking men as wolf bait and call it a distraction.'

'We've all been busy getting a big dose of Go and do as you're fucking told Kirk. This is what it looks like.' Said Chess

'Yes. Of course. That's it. I needed to go and tell you to recover the body of a man we've been working alongside of for months.' Jake was assiduously looking at the ground between his feet. Kirk looked at all the people around the fire and said. 'What I really want to know is when did all of you people start taking stupid pills.'

At that moment, having found the matches in the stores tent, Reece lit up the rag and threw it in the slit in the canvas. The anxiety that nothing would happen barely lasted a second as she threw herself face first into the snow and a huge 'whomp' sounded as the gases ignited and quickly set most surfaces in the tent on fire.

By the time the men around the campfire had begun to react she was in the garage shed, stopping long enough to splash some fuel on the battery bank and throw another fuel soaked rag on them leaving a half empty fuel can leaning beside them. Next she ran to the generator shed and, like the stores, was conflicted, but she was still taking on four men at least with the garage having two empty spaces suggesting there were more. She opened the main fuel storage tank valve and watched for a moment as the fuel came pouring out onto the snow. She ran to the generator and smashed the control panel with wrench liberated from the bench in the garage with five good belts being as much as her strength would allow to try to make in unrepairable. The machine chugged down to silence. She didn't dare light up the fuel pouring out of the main fuel tank as it might turn into a bomb that would tear her to pieces.

Now she had to execute what she thought one of the most dangerous parts of her plan. A clash of animals she had to put herself in the middle of. What she'd had to eat and drink was struggling to fuel a body which had the sweat freeze all over her because the furs she wore were made for someone thin rather than skeletal. She recovered her shaft and a bag of Davey meat from nearby.

She had a little dried meat as she ran and was hoping to sit down and have a real meal with Jake. As two free people. Or dying in the attempt to achieve that end. However she hadn't heard what she'd hoped to hear. So she saw her chances diminishing.

Meanwhile Kirk was shouting. He could not believe he'd been taken in by a scrawny girl. She and the man only a few feet away who had played him were going to pay and he didn't care who knew about it. 'Get the extinguishers. Go. If we can cut off the oxygen we can salvage it.' He didn't care about the stores. He wanted them occupied while he got the pistol. As Kirk said this all the lights went out as the battery bank caught fire and the generator died soon after. This was beyond belief. That misguided, petulant, and he'd assumed stupid girl, was only front for something much darker. There was only going to be one person walk away from this camp. Him. And now he needed every action focused on that outcome.

Chess had leapt up. He was going to release the dogs and follow them to find Reece. He had his own darkening plan for her. She would be disabled and dealt with last. He wasn't going to help put out any fires and he wasn't going to let the two mysterious wanderers work together either.

However Jake saw Chess coming and had enough presence of mind to move his head away from the blow. Chess was losing strength along with blood. He saw Jake go down and would be back to finish him off soon enough.

The hunter who had loved only his dog would treat his wounds once she was lying in the snow tied up. Her antler staff wouldn't work on these dogs because they were accustomed to barking at wild animals from a distance to signal their location and try to hold them in place that way. He assumed she must have run away from the camp from the back because she'd visited the generator shed. He let the two dogs off but kept them in control. They wanted to run but they were well enough trained. Not as well as Clive. Davey spent the time he wasn't working in the processing room with these dogs. And they were more accustomed to being controlled by the man whose intended violence towards Jake was not his natural reaction, but a response to what he's seen happen to Bertram and the attempt on his life. They came across tracks on the snow sooner than he expected. She hadn't run away from the camp. She'd run around behind it. And she was dragging something that no command from him was going to have any effect on.

He realised, again too late, what she was trying to do and so he called them off.

She was dragging the shirt she'd cut off the big man's body with a piece of his thigh in it. As he called there were two explosions in rapid succession in the stores tent that made him duck reflexively. Claude and Doc were emptying the contents of fire extinguishers into the narrow opening in the hanging canvas trying to push back the flames by directing the extinguishers onto the stores. Many of the boxes having burned off around melting contents in under a minute. The flames had run across the boxes more slowly where they hadn't been drenched in fuel. However once they reached the first fuel can it exploded creating a huge flash in addition to shrapnel from the can, followed by two more. The force of the explosion killed Doc and Claude instantly. It knocked Kirk down and gave him first degree burns all over his exposed skin as he turned to look at the two men facing into the fire on his way to getting his gun. He felt like he'd been baked. He gave a start in fright as the battery bank fuel can exploded.

Jake was laying on his side in the slush around the campfire As the radiant heat rolled over him it curled and singed his long hair and beard in a familiar sensation.

Reece felt a wave of relief to hear the explosions. She had no idea what damage it had done but hoped that it had disabled some of the men but not Jake.

She had hoped he would refuse to help put out the fire, however there was a nagging fear she had hurt or killed him. If nothing else she denied some stores and destroyed any chance they would have to keep killing animals this year. She was running as fast as she could, but that was only a little faster than someone well fed might walk. Boo Boo would still be roaming free if this had been the fastest she could run back then. As it happened, she had to slow down to get the timing right. She didn't want to arrive among a pack of feeding wolves and then wait for a pair or vicious dogs, but she couldn't move away in case they turned towards her. She started throwing pieces of meat she would rather have eaten in front of her as far as she could and walked closer to the feeding pack. She threw it between dogs and to the right and left of Davey's body to try to distracted them from her.

After a while she decided that due to the sounds the pack was making, she was unlikely to hear the dogs approaching and there was always the chance they would not have been released. She gave up and dropped the shirt and its grisly contents a half a dozen yards from his body and went to the tree the plan required her to climb. She was trying to do this to get above them as she heard the dogs arrive. She realised there was no prospect of her pulling herself even a foot off the ground.

She gripped her antler encrusted spear and readied herself. Two dogs, running at full speed along a confusing mix of scents were too close to the pack to turn on her trail and they smashed onto the scrum of wolves around Davy's body.

The sound that followed was beyond any dog fight she could imagine. The entire wolf pack turned their attention to the two intruders. Reece stopped, beathing heavily and chewed the last piece of meat she had. She was exhausted. Even if she and Jake could get away, if they were unable to steal some food and blankets she was finished. That would be okay. Together. They kicked the worst kind of wolf in the ass. Even if it was only one good kick, they would laugh, go as far as they could and then, she would suggest; bury themselves in the snow. They'd have one last laugh. At the hunger, cold, wolves, and then the worst predators of all. The disappointment of the hope they were perhaps unwise to embrace. They would laugh. Nothing could stop them doing that.

She pushed herself to go back to the camp. She could not force herself to run. It was the last piece of her plan and was the part that frightened her the most. She was so weak she worried she lacked the strength to do the very simple, mechanical actions needed to execute it.

She would look at who was left. If there were too many, she would turn and run as far as she could and bury herself. There were no dogs to track her. It would be over. She knew any laugh she would muster would be forced. As she walked to the camp, she rekindled the anger. They had tried so hard. And at the end only to cross paths with the worst kind of animal. If the leader of the pack or the odious Chess were there, she'd try her plan with them and then, she would save the last few blows for herself if Jake was gone. They weren't going to take her alive. But she was not going to let these nasty mean pathetic twisted fucks get away from her wrath.

Chess had turned off the torch. He looked into the darkness. His anger was building to a rage he had never experienced the like of; and he looked into his own darkness. He waited long enough to hear what he expected to hear. The sound of two dogs running headlong into a wolfpack. He turned back to get his gun set next to his pack behind the tents. Like Reece. He was weakening fast. Like Reece he was relying on anger to sustain himself.

When Reece arrived at the camp she saw Doc and Claude lying on their backs. She saw Jake lying on his side. Head in the slush. Facing her. His eyes were closed, and she assumed he was dead. Kirk was standing looking at the stores burn. His face bathed in the light of the fames.

194

She hated him and the feeling was mutual. He turned around to look at her. His face still red even not reflected the fire.

She would finish what she started or die trying. She was strangely relaxed because she believed he would kill quickly from the pure rage in his eye. That might be better than lying in the snow.

So she helped his rage along. 'How do you like me now Kirk.' She almost hissed this. Looking him in the eye. She had never felt anything like this. Kirk for all his experience of some of the most mercenary people on the planet was looking into the eyes of a sixteen-year-old who had completely torn apart his operations and substantially destroyed his life and prospects and would not stop until her heart did.

He gazed into her eyes. He saw her mind and wanted her to be sure she could not be more wrong about suffering a quick death at his hands. 'It was going to be painless Reece. Not any more. And I have all the time in the world now.'

That should have undercut her confidence, but she was committed now, and her plan was simplicity itself as long as she achieved one simple thing. He surged towards.

She contrived a look which suggested she'd miscalculated terribly. She called out. 'No.' And ran. Appearing terrified. This was not too difficult a response to portray in the circumstances. Kirk could still not know she was someone who knew she could only ever outwit him. Never out power him.

Had he not been feeling the pain of burning skin, eyes watering, anger boiling and revenge plans forming he might have noticed she didn't carry the weapon he had heard had been so effective. She was turning to watch him as he approached. She wanted to make sure when he reached out to grab her, he didn't enclose her arms in the embrace of the inevitable tackle and ideally not around the neck, though she could manage that.

He came into range, and she flung her arms out as if she was going to try to jump forward. He locked his arms around her mid-section initially and she stopped suddenly causing him to need to concentrate on not falling forward. She didn't struggle in the least as he steadied himself then leaned back to lift her off her feet. When they'd walked towards the camp she'd had four 'dagger sticks' pushed under her belt which now had many new holes to keep it tight. These were the sharp sticks they used to stab an injured animal if they had speared it, and it needed to be caught and killed.

Also as a last defence against attack by a wolf after casting or losing their spears.

Now she had one in each fist. Before he caught her, pointing backwards along her forearm. Once he grasped her, she pushed them through her clenched fist against her thighs so they pointed back towards Kirk and she started driving her fists backwards and forwards, gripping the wooden spikes tightly. Aiming behind her head and stabbing backwards as quickly and violently as she could. Slightly upwards to accommodate his greater height.

Chess had emerged with his gun as she was being caught This was perfect for him. Both were about to die. Kirk quickly. She was going to take several hits in the leg to make sure she was incapacitated. The other wayfarer would also get a bullet if he needed one. He would come up with credible stories as to what happened. Including what was going to happen to the two hunters in the morning who had shown him only disrespect.

The dagger sticks were eight inches long and three quarter of an inch thick in the middle and tapered to a fire hardened point. She was pushing them back behind her head so fast and forcefully she made a quarter inch rip in the top of her own ear.

She didn't know where Kirk positioned his head but she was stabbing over her shoulder and upwards behind and to the left and right of her head, which she was holding forward to ensure she was stabbing directly behind herself. She felt several jarring hits as she punctured somewhere on Kirk's face to the bone. He was too enraged to drop her and tried to move his head away and squeezed her hard which achieve nothing. Then he released one of his arms, the other locked around her, and captured one of hers and pulled it into his vice grip. He was about to do the same on the other side when she felt one stick spear into soft tissue five inches further than the others and she let go of it.

Chess had found it difficult to aim because Kirk was moving his head around once he was confronted with sharp sicks flying at him. He then saw that as unlikely as it was, she was going to do the job for him. It made him feel good. He had been derided for letting this 'scrawny kid' outsmart him and so it was fitting that she executed the last thing she was going to be allowed to get away with. Once Kirk had a stick buried in his eye Chess was lifting the gun to take aim. He felt a hand grab him roughly by the hair on the back of his head and another gouging its fingers pushing deep into the wounded shoulder.

He tried to spin around however Jake had some momentum but most effectively he was driving both his knees hard into the back of Chess's knees and leaned forward with his full weight. Irrespective of how weak the rancher was, they were both destined to fall over. Jake would easily be flung off and beaten to death, so he had come from an angle and twisted Chess as they fell so the hunter, his eyes locked on Reece, didn't appreciate he was pointing exactly where Jake wanted him to land. It took Chess a second to drop his gun and throw his hands forward to catch himself. His hands landed in four-inch-deep coals at either edge of the campfire. These were all that held him off the centre of the dying flames fed by a deep bed of coals. His face was being licked at by the flames of the fire and his beard started melting. Jake knew he had seconds. Chess was about to twist and throw him off. However gripping Chess's head hard with a handful of hair and driving two fingers deeper into the wound in his shoulder, Jake, like everyone around that fire, was furious. In one motion he pushed off with his toes and pulled his knees up and as far forward as he could and drove them into the middle of Chess's back as he thrashed violently in a lunge to break free. Chess was struggling to twist without landing in the fire. Jakes knees pushed him down and forward in a jolt so his arms buckled, and his face went into coals.

The screaming escaping from among the deep coals was a strange sound. Jake was about to swing his focus to going to Reece's assistance however the fact Chess's hair and clothes were catching fire caused him to make an awkward retreat from the burning man's back. He half stood, then staggered back and tripped over one bench, saved himself, staggered further and the fell over a chair and landed heavily in the slush.

He was going to get straight up but he heard Reece speaking. In a strange voice. She was kneeling over a man who was moaning. An uncoordinated hand groping around a wooden spike deep in his eye.

She'd taken his knife and held him by the hair. Jake heard her say. 'What do you call a deer with no eyes?'

Kirk's string of unintelligible sounds modulated a little.

'Wrong answer.' She slit his throat as Jake had taught her and let his head fall. His hands groped briefly and fell back.

Jake found it convenient to hold a singed hand and what had been the singed part of his beard and hair in the slush for a moment because he wanted her to come and help him up as the concluding act of what he thought was a remarkable attack against a camp of bad men and hunting dogs while turning wolves into her allies.

He saw a pair of fur covered boots appear in front of him. More fur stuffed in them to stop them sliding off.

It was time to maintain the tone. Their approach. They both knew it. Never take life and their adventure too seriously. 'That guy is toast.' Said Reece. Nodding towards Chess and laughing. She held out her hand. She knew Jake was fine to get up on his own and this was his way of showing respect.

He took it and stood up. 'And you gave the bad guys what they deserved. We were made for this stuff Reece.' He slapped her on the back like he would do one of the men he'd hire seasonally on the ranch.

'A bit scary really.' There was a trace in there of an anxiety which she knew would grow to plague her mind. She'd leave that for later though. 'A shame about Clive. He sounded like he was okay.'

'Young lady there's a lesson for Clive and all of us there about falling in with the wrong crowd.' Said Jake in a voice an adult with unassailable authority might use when speaking to a child in need of some life coaching.

Reece nodded and nudged Chess with her book. 'There's a lesson here as well. Smoking is bad for you.'

They laughed again. They were both coming down from an adrenaline rush that could land in one of a few ways. They were grateful to each other it was laughter. They looked at the stores tent at the same time. Still burning strongly, the tent itself fully ablaze so that they were lit up even with no electricity. It was enough radiant heat to get them both feeling warm. 'Shame I burned all the stores.'

'They might have a kitchen where they have a few things. Or some leftovers. I had a nice hot meal while you were making a deal with wolves. I could eat again though. About five more times.'

'Vegetables. Who would have thought I am hoping there are even a few vegetables left.'

'Let's go and see.'

It was almost as satisfying to find some left over stew which had some carrots and potatoes in it as executing a plan she never believed would work. They came out to see that the flames were dying down in the stores tent. There was a mixture of enticing smells and the smell of some things burning that weren't supposed to burn. Especially plastic.

Two men lay on their back with their faces smashed in. Another had bled out with a stake in his eye.

Reece went to the woodpile and put some medium sized pieces of timber over Chess's head and shoulders. She knitted her brows and looked at Jake. 'Are we bad people?'

'No way.' Said Jake. 'We're the good guys. I'll show you why.' Jake thought she'd asked in jest, however he wanted her to see what had been saved in addition to themselves. 'I haven't been in here, but I have a good idea what we'll find.' When they opened one half of the double doors they were at once fascinated and disgusted. They had thanked the No I-deer and Boo Boo for saving them. As they had done with all the smaller and less memorable creatures they'd caught and eaten. They'd thanked the wolves for not killing them. Here there were scores of skins, pelts, antlers and taxidermy trophy heads of all kinds of animals.

'This is wrong. Pure and simple.' Said Reece.

'You went way too easy on those guys Reece.'

She looked at her older travelling companion. 'The people who order this…they aren't going to get these. No one should.'

'Except for two.'

'Two?'

'Wolf Girl, how many animals do you think you saved tonight? They said they were halfway through their season. And they'd be back next year. Maybe after a season somewhere else in the world. Quite a few animals who are now going to die of natural causes would be happy for you to pick one thing. I know what I want if there is one.'

They walked around and started to look though the stacks. It was sickening to be looking through a stack of wolf skins thirty high. She was also having trouble choosing. Jake was wandering around the edges. He knew what he wanted. Though a piece of him was hoping it wasn't there. He wished these skins were still wrapped around the animals as they were supposed to be.

He shook his head and said to himself. 'A lot of these animals are shot like cattle in a pasture.' He found what he was looking for. There was a section of the room with wide shelves. It was where they kept the high-end merchandise. Before he pulled his off the shelf he said. 'I found yours.'

She came over to see a skin from a large wolf. The fur was in a beautiful pattern of white and grey and the face and tail had been carefully skinned and preserved. Reece immediately fell in love with it. 'Now I can die of exposure happy. It's Wolf Girl that will have left the building.'

She looked up to see Jake draping the large shaggy coat of a grizzly bear over his shoulders. Reece motioned him to bend down so she could put the bears head on top of his. It had glass eyes and the snout and upper set of teeth preserved.

'Bear phobia be damned.' He said.

'It's time for the world to be afraid of what…Bear Man.'

'That doesn't quite hit the right…tone.'

'Bear Guy.'

'A little better.'

Jake danced around a little. He wasn't much good at dancing, but it worked wearing a Grizzly bear skin.

'Dancing Bear Guy.' She said.

He smiled. 'A bit of practice and I will own that name.'

Reece spent some time looking around while Jake got to work cutting strips of leather and putting holes in their respective skins so they could tie the heads on like a bonnet and have a few holes down the front to tie them on like a coat. He tried his on a few times to get the lengths of leather right so he could have it held around himself. The two edges that had been the bears belly joined up and got him fully enclosed.

He decided to make a few ties though the skin at the bears wrist and elbow so he could tie the bear's arms to his. Including paws and claws. Reece helped. She wanted the same treatment as much as her skin would allow. She was so thin the wolf skin nearly made it all the way around. Jake gave her a chin strap and a heavier leather tie at the base of her neck and one over each shoulder and under her arms so that if she took the ties off under her chin it hung as a cape.

'I can say with absolute certainty I am never taking this off. I haven't felt so warm in years.' Said Jake.

'And you look terrifying.'

'That's right. Until I start dancing. Which I intend to do a lot of.'

'Do you think if I ever go back to school I'll get teased for being Wolf Girl.'

'I am absolutely certain you will. Until people start disappearing.'

'Yeah. And the really mean ones will get their face all messed up with the Staff of Justice first.' Reece said this while looking though boxes of glass eyes.

They saw dressing up in animal skins as a perfectly normal way to wind down after killing six men and three dogs. Making an allowance for the fact that a pack of wolves counted as being on their team.

Reece was fascinated by the eyes in various boxes. There were a range that she imagined were for everything from bears to moose. 'Are you thinking what I'm thinking?' She held up some glass eyes.

Jake was still in the last conversation. 'That you might be changing schools frequently?'

'No I was wondering how these would look.'

'Do we need to take dressing up as animals that far?'

'No. Come on.' She went outside to where Kirk lay. 'He doesn't look so good.' Reece looked at what were probably the glass eyes for a moose in her hand and hesitated.

'The bear whose skin I'm wearing happens to be a trifle annoyed with Kirk.' He didn't want to see Reece back down. He pulled out the dagger stick from one of Kirk's eyes and then, much more clumsily than he'd hoped, held on to one of the bear's claws and scooped out the uninjured eye, which sat framed in a dozen puncture wounds all around his face and neck.

The two empty sockets exposed were gruesome. Especially since the poacher had an unnaturally red face and gave them both pause.

However Reece was glad that Jake had made it so that she didn't have decide it was a bad idea. She bent down and pushed the glass eyes in hard. They popped into the sockets in a surprisingly satisfying way. They both stood back to look at their handywork in the glow of the fire. 'That's creepy. He was a creepy guy already but now…'

'Dancing Bear Guy loves Kirk's new look.' Kirk looked back with what appeared to be jet black eyes. 'It's what he would have like to do himself had he not taken on Wolf Girl and got himself killed.' They dumped more wood on Chess and made some jam and cheeses sandwiches to eat by the fire. The strange mood continued.

Dancing Bear Guy nodded towards Kirk. 'Poor guy was only trying to give us a job.'

'Damn. I forgot about that. Are we bad people?'

'No way. Look at the nice pair of eyes we gave him. I suspect all these people were on the brink of having a…what do you call it…'

'No I Deer.' Said Wolf Girl

'…yeah… I know what they were about to have…epiphany.' Jake's university days and wide reading diet broke through into his emaciated mind in the strange setting. 'All these people were going to have one and realise what terrible things they'd done. They were going to feel bad their whole life long. We came along and saved them from that.'

'Ha. I heard that word a few months back when a certain asshole was telling me how he realised…ha ha…he was an asshole.'

Jake was reflective. 'It's the circle of Karma closing.'

'I didn't know Karma was circular.'

'I'm not an expert. I simply assumed it wasn't square.' Jake then remembered something. Oh…yeah. That reminds me. Karma. That other guy.'

'Other guy?'

'You know the second guy you jabbed with the Staff of Justice thing.'

'I forgot about him. Is he…'

'I think he's still alive. In that tent…hut thing over there.'

'Oh.' Brows knitted under a wolf face. 'I'm trying to figure out if that's a good thing or a bad thing. I'm probably supposed to feel like that it would be a good thing. If I was honest with myself however I'd say I think it would be a bad thing. Are your sure we're not bad people?'

'No way. That guy…the guy you…mutilated I guess you'd call it; I think he's the one who stuck the glass eyes in Dancing Bear Guy's head.'

'Once he has his epiphany he's going to feel terrible.'

It was dawning on them how inconvenient a mutilated taxidermist would be. 'We should go and see if he's okay.'

They went to the hut and walked in a little tentatively. They didn't conceal their relief when they realised there was no one left alive. Neither would be quite sure what to do with a man in pain who they were ambivalent about. If he was a nice guy that was going to present a whole range of problems. Fortunately they were confronted by a man killed by Kirk. Bertram was not going to make it in any event.

Dancing Bear Guy had to start laughing again when Wolf Girl looked across and said. 'Are you...'

'This time I do know what you're thinking.'

'I saw some blue ones that must be for wolves. Do wolves have blue eyes. I've been up close a few times now, but I've never looked them in the eye.'

'I don't know but I think it doesn't matter because some people are going to want their wolf head with blue eyes.'

'Cheaters. That's another example of how much people like that really annoy me. Don't even care about what you call it. Authenticness. Jesus my brain is fried.'

Going back into the merchandise room they were distracted for a while looking around at things they hadn't seen the first time. Eventually they were back in front of Bertram. Jake had remembered his name which Reece said she thought was a nice name. It was awkward getting the remains of his eyes out. One of Kirk's was gone and the other came out whole. Both Bertram's were a bit mushy. Dancing Bear Guy eventually went for spoon.

The blue glass eyes were slightly too small but once Reece straightened them they stood back and both nodded.

'I have no doubt Bertram was annoyed that I...mushed up his eyes. Now I think he'd be very pleased with where things landed.'

'Maybe we should get a mirror so he can...no that's not going to work.' Said Jake.

'That's right dancing Bear Guy. He won't be able to see anything because they're glass.'

While Jake was saying this Reece was adjusting them so they looked towards a point six inches beyond his face. 'I'm really hungry again.' She said.

Jake looked around the various beds. 'I'd say the guy who took up smoking out there would be the kind to have some things hidden away for late at night or things he didn't want anyone else to know he had.'

'I'd feel a lot better if I didn't burn all the food. Given that 'moose eyes' out there said we're still a long way from anywhere. And...'

'And?'

'The guy in the fireplace is way over cooked now.'

They were pulling open the locker next to Chess's bed and then removing the things that were in a burlap bag containing chocolate, a half-eaten container of peanut butter and a quarter jar of strawberry jam plus a particular spice Chess liked in large quantities on his food. Which had been a further annoyance to Claude.

212

'I need to warn you Jake that this guy didn't use a spoon.'

'That's a concern.'

They both laughed. 'Who are we kidding.' After a few serves of stew their bodies could tolerate some chocolate and peanut butter and jam in small doses. Reece saw a long blank cardboard box and drew out a bottle still a third full of brown liquid. 'What do you think Dancing Bear Guy. Celebration time.'

Jake could not help but allow the mood to slide to where his reactions took them. He was shaking his head sadly. 'I nearly lost may ranch because of that stuff Reece. And I…well I did lose what was the most important thing to me.'

She wanted to help Jake move past that. So she spoke like the authority figure to the innocent child. 'There's a lesson in that Dancing Bear Guy. Stick to the psychedelics. Which I'm pretty sure Chess doesn't have any of.' She changed the subject. 'How about we see what's in the bosses office.'

They walked in and were immediately confronted by something which created a huge challenge. It was a radio. And sitting on the desk was a phone. It was a large phone in a robust case. 'I reckon if we knew the password we could pick up that phone and call just about anybody.'

'Yeah.' They each took a chair. They weren't looking at each other and thinking the same thing which did happen more and more as they had travelled and needed to make decisions silently. What they were thinking was that they wanted to be able to get warm when they wanted to. Or at least when they needed to. And they wanted enough food so they were in good shape, or at least enough so they weren't skin and bone. But they didn't want the adventure to end. Not because they didn't miss the comforts of home, and, though less than they expected, the lives they had. But because they wanted to finish what they'd started. What they'd been forced to start. Only one of the motivations was to prove to the dead Russel Hansen that they refused to accept the fate he thought he could assign them. They wanted to finish it because they had taken life on. And now had a chance to win. Or perhaps collaborate with it on good terms. So strange as it was, given they had been on the threshold of dying from exposure a few hours before, they had no ideas as to who to call.

'Shame we can't.' Concluded Reece.

'By the look of that radio it's a short-range signal anyhow. We have a similar system on the Ranch. Here I'd say they want something intentionally short range.' It reminded him of something, and he had some sobering news to impart.

'Before he got his moose eyes fitted, I heard Kirk calling in some of his men. There's at least two more people out there.'

Reece pursed her lips. A concern had been growing in her mind. 'You know Dancing Bear Guy this isn't fair. We defend ourselves like anybody would and now I imagine we're going to get in a whole bunch of trouble like we did something wrong.' Reece shook her wolf clad head. 'It isn't right.'

'I hear you. It isn't.'

'Are you thinking what I'm thinking.'

Dancing Bear Guy looked across at her. 'I'll be honest with you Wolf Girl. Right then I wasn't thinking about anything. Except maybe roasted beetroot. The question is, why was I thinking about roasted beet root. I don't cook it at home.'

'I was thinking we burn this sucker down. Everything. Get what we can from the ashes of the store as far as food goes. Get some of their backpacks. Warm clothes and whatever. Burn it all to the ground and if… I mean when we get out of here, we know nothing about some bad people killing off animals. Hell I'm ready to forget the whole thing and move on.'

'We get what we need and leave not a trace we were ever here. Let's see if there's any more extinguishers to put those stores out completely and let them cool down. I'm certain there's going to be some good stuff left in there and they might have a separate store of meat but if we can get a gun we can get some meat from a distance. We'd have to say thank you from a distance is all.'

'Let's do it. We've got a lot to do because it sounds like those...' She laughed. 'What do you call them on the ranch. Those varmints are heading this way. If they get going by first light, we should be planning on being gone by not too long after.' They were both exhausted and this was impacting their ability to make accurate assessments and also apparently caused them to laugh at things much more then was deserved. 'What is a varmint Dancing Bear Guy.'

'I'm not exactly sure. Everyone we've come across here is one though. Except Bertram. I get the feeling that fella made a bad decision. Under the influence of varmints I don't doubt.'

'There's a lesson in that Dancing Bear Guy. He got a pair of nice blue wolf eyes out of the deal which I think Kirk is probably quite jeal... whoa do you see that!' Reece interrupted herself. There was an external battery pack for the phone. She picked it up and pressed a button.

Three of the four lights were green. She held it up. 'Are you thinking what I'm thinking.' Jake knew it couldn't be about a signal to make a call on their phones. And there was no one left to put glass eyes into. Or so he thought at that juncture. 'Tunes. We can play some tunes. You're the Dancing Bear Guy and I'm your partner in…um…getting justice for innocent animals. We can dance to some tunes.' She looked around the desk for cables and found some in a drawer and pulled out her phone for her bag which Chess had carried in. 'All is forgiven technophobic bear.' While her phone was charging enough to turn on they started to look through the cupboards and drawers in Kirks office. There was a door leading off the office and inside was a small room with a bed and a locker in it. Kirk didn't sleep with the help. There were some high-quality thermals they shared out and Jake went out to the office so they could both put them on without sparing the time to talk about it. She brought out thick socks, some boots that would fit Jake and more clothes they both started to put on. If they found better clothes in the other rooms they'd keep putting them on top. She would find later, with three pairs of socks, Bertram's boots were a good fit

Reece saw that her phone was on and she looked at the passcode. 'Can you believe this. I have no idea…'

'Don't you mean No I De…'

'Actually that's not for day-to-day use. It's my new…damn. What do you call it. My brain is fried.'

'Catch phrase.'

'Yeah. Catch phrase. Not that I expect to use it again.' She frowned and squinted at the phone as if that would fix the passcode problem. 'I guess when you attack wolves to steal their food passcodes get tossed out of your brain.'

'Birthday?'

She smiled. 'Nope. But now I remember.' She brought up her playlist and held the phone out to Jake. 'Dancing Bear Guy. It's your pick. One tune a day till we get back. We'll take turns.'

Jake smiled. His anxiety that there would be nothing he would recognise was short lived. There were a lot of songs he knew. Partly because Wolf Girl had eclectic tastes, and also he had always had younger people on the ranch helping out and absorbed some of their music. He scrolled through and picked something which he believed could not be more appropriate. 'I'm Feeling Good' in the case the Micheal Bublé version. Wolf Girl's eyes lit up. Neither of them had done much dancing. And they had never danced together.

They were moving around and laughing, making the kinds of clawing and loping movements they thought the kind of fauna they had taken the personas of might do.

They were breathing heavily. 'I have not been this warm since I...I can't remember. Let's go and find some more to eat and then we need to get to work. We have a lot to do before sunrise. To get some of these places to burn, like where they have all the skins and trophies, we'll need to bring in some wood. I think I burned or wasted all the fuel in the place. And that part of the plan, though it's not a great outcome now, was mainly so if we died, and least they were cold and hungry because of us.'

They had some sandwiches and began bringing some of the cut wood into the merchandise hut. They were both blinking and yawning. Reece had experienced an intense six hours towards the end of what they thought might be their last day alive. Jake had been knocked out briefly twice but had also been awake much longer than they were used to. Adding these things together he was feeling his age a little. Irrespective of the need to push south, they were so exhausted they had grown used to sleeping as soon as it was dark until the light woke them, as with other animals who had the misfortune to need to stay awake through the winter months. 'Maybe we should sleep for an hour.'

'I'll set my alarm.' Neither wanting to admit an hour was a ludicrous amount of sleep to allow them to burn a camp down, stock up and leave the area with barely five hours until sunrise.

'Yeah.' She got her phone and set the alarm. Not realising the battery had been through such hardship it was drained to exhaustion soon after she took it off the power source. They each chose a pile of skins as a bed and threw one on top, even though they didn't need it as they had such warm clothes and Reece turned off the lanterns that were positioned all through the camp.

Although Reece missed Boo Boo, hidden in a tree away from the wolves, they both fell into a sleep they'd not had since even before their adventure started because they'd never been so exhausted and then had the chance to rest, have plenty of food, be warm and feel safe. This last feeling evaporated when they both woke up at the same time, looked around to see it was light. They were awoken by voices. They looked at each other and went to a corner of the room behind a stack of skins near the wall. Reece looked at Jake. 'Are we stupid people?'

'Um…yeah I think we might be. We're well rested stupid people though.'

'That's going to count. Now that I think about it, they would probably come after us in those snow…running on top of…machines.'

'Oh yeah. Those.'

'You know what they're called.'

'Snowmobiles.'

'I needed to know. It would have annoyed me. Is this what it's like when you get old.'

'Who's old. I'm Dancing Bear Guy.'

'Oh yeah. And you're the one who remembers words. And getting a bunch of rest means maybe we're not stupid people.'

'I'm sure we're not.'

'Phew.'

They looked at each other and both made the 'shh' sign with their fingers and tried not to laugh.

The voices were moving around the camp. They heard one calling from a distance after a while. They were further away and then approached. The bear and wolf incarnations shared a silent decision to remain hidden until they were certain they could escape.

That brief look included waiting until they could steal a few things on the way out or there was no point. They were both used to waiting for quarry to emerge from holes or caves or trees. Or for storms to pass, for two days recently. They were good at sitting quietly now.

The door opened and one man arrived and went to the bench. He was looking though the boxes of eyes on the table and the dozen eyes Reece had set out in pairs when she was choosing them for Kirk and later Bertram. An activity now, after ten hours of sleep, for which she felt a twinge of regret. Only a brief twinge though. Another man came in and the two voices were clear. One had an accent Jake knew to be South African and the other a broad accent from the Southern US. 'You find Davey?'

'What was left of him. The wolves made a mess of that guy and his dogs. Fred and Ginger aren't a pretty sight. They took a wolf with them though. It was like it had half its coat burned off. Probably on the way out anyway.'

Dancing Bear Guy's eyes locked onto Wolf Girl's with a look of boyish excitement.

'I followed some tracks and found Clive. Had a big stick rammed so deep down his throat it nearly came out his asshole.'

'Damn. I loved that dog. Even if his owner was a dick.'

'Yeah well they roasted his head off. And guess what.'

'What?'

'He must have gone in alive. I looked at his hands. They were burned to a crisp before he eventually fell forward and they got pushed out sideways. Must have been trying to hold himself up.'

'Jesus. There's more to the Davey story. It wasn't the wolves that got him. He had a big hole under his chin with another one in the back of his head. He got speared like Clive.'

'And the eyes in Kert and Bertram.'

'Who mutilates somebody and then puts glass eyes into them. I imagine they would have done Doc and Claude if their faces weren't so badly smashed up.'

'What kind of sick, perverted people are we dealing with here?'

Reece made an angry face at Jake under the wolf face. Which also appeared a little put upon, as if the predator was on the verge of going and telling his side of the story.

'From our point of view, they burned most of the stores and fried the batteries. Used most of the fuel cans as bombs. We can get every container we can find we might be able to hold enough to get out of here. I don't know if we'll make…must be over five hundred miles.'

'And what do we do when we get there. No passports, no ID, no money. The assholes who set this up want us to stay the course and stick to that confidentiality oath or whatever it was we signed.'

'Or we end up mounted on the wall.'

'I think about that sometimes. It wouldn't surprise me if some of the rich pricks we ultimately work for don't have a basement full of human heads mounted the same way as they have the bear and tiger heads on the wall they were too lazy to come and shoot for themselves.'

'This is a mess. We have to consider that the sick…psychos who came, apparently out of nowhere and did this…we don't know how much they know. They've been right through Kirk's stuff. Who knows what they took. Maybe he had the contracts we never saw again. Or copies of our papers. There's no tracks of any snowmobiles or anything else they might travel with.'

'They must be crazy people who somehow live out here and once they found this place they played out some twisted fantasy. When the authorities eventually find this place…I mean hell it looks like they tortured Kirk and Bertram, and who knows what they did to Chess before they burned his head off. Those people might know way more than is good for us.' The southerner scratched his head. 'And…shit. People might even blame us.'

The South African was still musing about the one good outcomes of this. 'Burning that assholes head off is the one thing they did I'm okay with. Of course that's a hindsight thing. I would have liked to burn that guy's head right off his fucking shoulders but I would never have dreamed up something that nasty.'

'We need to stick together and keep an eye out.' Reece nearly laughed at the eye out reference. 'What's interesting is they didn't use any firearms. Maybe they don't have any. Let's go and fuel up then we'll start searching. Unlike the poor suckers outside we know what we're dealing with.'

'Yep. And we've run down half of the sneaky, mean, dangerous animals on the planet.'

The man with the South African accents said. 'Whatever happens I'm taking a few of these with me.'

'Once I figure out how to get myself out of this freezing country half a dozen of the best of these will cover what I was supposed to get paid and then some.' He started to look through the pile. His searches became more and more earnest. 'It's not here. The best hide this operation got. My white wolf. There's not many of those left. It took me a week to bring that wily fella down.' He gave a short bark of laughter. 'He eventually came out for his mate. Like she'd come out for her pups when I caught them. She had a good hide too but his was the best I've ever seen. Huge.' Neither felt obliged to follow Kirk's rules to leave an animal with cubs, pups or calves to maintain stocks for future seasons.

The other man was looking around only a few meters from where they hid behind the tallest stack. Reindeer hides. He was now also aggrieved. 'We only got one Grizzly hide this season so far and that's gone too.'

'These fucking people. They're not satisfied with killing everyone. They have to take the best hides.'

'It's another reason we need to run whoever did this down. Hides like those are worth fifty times that of the ordinary ones. And a lot less bulky to get across a border.'

They left and when the two people under very valuable hides heard the snowmobiles start up Reece and Jake knew it was time to make a move. Wolf Girl said. 'Are we sick twisted people.'

'No way.' Said Dancing Bear Guy. 'The whole thing's a big misunderstanding. No point in trying to explain it though Anyway, those guys go all round the world killing for trophies. How's that for sick and twisted. We're the good guys in this story.'

'That's right. Going around the world killing beautiful animals for rich people. Not people I'd strike up a friendship with. Plus the fact they want to kill us.'

'An important detail Wolf Girl.'

Once they heard the snow mobiles drive over to the fuel tank Reece and Jake ran. She explained why they may not be there very long. They went into the utility room and found backpacks and took them to the stores room. They were surprised that some of it was still too hot to move around by hand even eight hours later, so they went for a snow pick and began to pull the upper boxes off. Mercifully there were some boxes at the very bottom that were unburned. It was possible some of the contents had boiled in the jars and cans, but they would take that chance.

The big find were some bags of rice in the bottom boxes. Pure carbohydrates. They would take two five kilogram bags each. They threw some condiments on the top and heard the machines start up. They realised they had five hundred miles left to go and with better knives they had a chance but knew what they really needed was a gun.

'Let's get into the woods and collect out thoughts.' Said Jake.

As they left the stores hut Reece said. 'Take my pack. I've got to get something. Don't wait.'

She turned to the side and went into the barracks hut. Jake was uncertain what to do but ran as far as the tree line.

A thought had struck Reece as they went through the remainder of the stores. Chess was a man who had certain preferences. He liked to have a drink in what was supposed to be a dry camp and liked strawberry jam so much they'd run out of it. He also liked something in his food much more than anyone else in the camp, so he kept his own supply. She'd seen it in his locker and now she wanted it.

'This is serious.' Said the South African. As if it needed to be stated.

'No fuel. Maybe a hundred miles out of each machine.'

'If we tip that tank right over we might get some more out of it, but it'll still be well short of what we need.' They were silent for a while. 'Shit. We haven't eaten since last night and I need a coffee. Let's pull Chess out of the God damn fire and make some breakfast.'

'Yeah. I better go back and turn the generator on. We're going to need what's in the refrigerators not to spoil. We can bypass the battery bank and have a direct feed.'

'Sure. We should think about walking places rather than use the snow mobiles unless we have to. Those things take a bit of fuel to kick over.'

'Good point.' The pair had always worked well together. Though now their interests were diverging. They were both having the same thought come to life like a flame licking at the surface of their minds. Even with all the fuel in one machine they wouldn't make it back. But they'd get much closer. They were both imagining a world where a single snow mobile loaded with the premium hides strapped to it went south.

Reece was listening at the barracks door. Once she heard the southerner leave, she waited until he would be out of earshot. She had laid the wolf hide over Bertram.

In the clear light of day she decided being a nice guy but spending your days stuffing beautiful dead animals weren't consistent and she was okay with the strange blue eyes he stared back at her with. She heard some sounds consistent with dragging a body out of a campfire and stepped out of the door and was able to get around the corner without being seen. She went some distance away and then ran back and came out into the open breathing heavily. 'Mister. Thank God you're here. I got away. I got away after all this time. Those…people they came and took me from a campground I was staying at it must be two years ago. They're…twisted…bad people. You need to let my parents know that I'm alright. Mister you need to get me out of here.'

She thought he might have been a little more sympathetic, but it didn't matter. He approached and she had positioned herself so that if he was going to grab her by the arm it would be the left arm. He did this and shook her. 'I don't know what's going on, but I need to hear everything you know and in a hurry.' He shook her hard at this last word. This was a major complication he could do without.

She looked him in the eye as she reached into her pocket. 'The main thing is…I don't like what you did to my puppies.'

As she was saying this, she had taken a handful of the chilli powder she'd put in her pocket. She'd ripped open five supermarket size bags from Chess's locker and put it in the high-quality jacket she liberated from Kirk's wardrobe the night before. She threw it in his eyes and turned away, wrenching her arm from his grip, keeping her eyes tight shut and breathing out of her nose. She had to fall to the ground to get free and she rolled over. She was on her feet as quickly as possible. He was standing with his fingers pressed into his eyes bending over and starting to tell her the things that were going to happen to her. Because he needed to open his mouth to vent this diatribe it gave her the opportunity to throw a handful in there also. Followed by three more, diminishing in size into his face, until he fell over gasping.

She knew she didn't have long. She was mad about the puppies though. And there was the whole catch phrase thing now, so she was quickly on her knees beside him. 'What do you call a deer with no eyes.'

The man made a sound which bore no resemblance to a word. 'Wrong answer.' Kirk's knife went to work once again. She looked up to see that Jake was at the edge of the fire on an errand of his own and he simply stopped, picked up a stone, looked and nodded. She nodded and ran after him.

Jake ran to the utility shed to get what he wanted and leaned it against the office hut. They smiled at each other as they prepared to climb.

The southerner arrived to find his partner's face covered in chilli powder and his throat slit. Although there was a tiny moment of relief that he would have all the fuel and so have a better chance of getting out, his main concern was that everyone in the camp had been killed. None with a gun and his partner within an hour of arriving. He got three guns from snow mobile. One a shotgun. It wasn't for trophies. It was for killing or frightening things that were a threat. Now it was to induce fear. And partly to alleviate some of his own. He wanted to let them know he was coming. He let off a shot which was resoundingly loud in the quiet winter air.

'You think you're going to kill me like you did the rest?' He was shouting and let off another shot. 'You got that wrong.' He was turning in a circle as he called out and reloaded. 'I've hunted most of the meanest, nastiest god damn animals on this planet and they're all smarter than you so don't expect an easy time of it.' He let off another shot and then another. 'Every animal leaves a trail, and they all have their weaknesses. I already figured out yours.' Another blast. 'So if I was you. I'd start running. Fast.'

A fist sized stone streaked through the air. Hit him on the head. And killed him.

Had there been anyone left alive, they would have heard two people having a big laugh on the top of a hut covered by a white tent. Of the myriad things the man hadn't known about Jake and Reece was that they had spent, before exhaustion took over, an inordinate amount of time throwing stones. First skipping stones on the water. A talent Jake was soon to freely admit Reece had an almost supernatural knack for. Then Jake had recalled the story of the friendly stone throwing ogres, and they made a game of it. One of them would pick up a stone. The other would call a random target for them to aim at. They didn't keep score but tried to designate targets similar distances and elevations to the those the animals they hunted were often seen at.

Eventually they realised that even though they did kill an occasional small animal, they were probably using more energy throwing stones than the gains they were making in calories. They enjoyed it so much though that they kept doing it, eventually needing to put themselves on a 'stone diet' which might vary depending on how much they had in their belly and in their skin bags.

They climbed down the ladder.

As with her pre-eminence with stone skipping, Jake was the master when it came to killing animals with fist sized stones. He had a power and accuracy Reece could never hope to emulate. He had eaten and was well rested so he'd had enough power behind a shot if it was accurate enough.

Standing over the man who thought a monologue would help his situation Reece said. 'I never got to ask him what a deer with no eyes was called.'

'I don't think he had the intelligence to know about things like that.'

'It's a good thing because a cracked head is what we needed for this one.'

'Oh?' Said Jake.

'He's the real bad guy. He was telling us what a great job he was going to do at killing us.'

'Are you thinking what I'm thinking.' Jake said. He knew Reece had developed a plan, but she would want to go through a process of seeing what he thought. He'd rather listen to what she thought without going through that.

'We take what we can carry...including him...on one of those...damn...drive over the snow things...with all the fuel in it. Everything else we burn.'

'Burn as hot as we can get it. Drive until we use up nearly all the fuel and then roll him and the machine off a cliff that he might be dumb enough not to see coming. We start walking out and if we make it, we've never heard of this place. Why should we get in trouble simply for passing through somewhere.'

Jake was beginning to understand the depth of Reece's anxiety about where they might end up should the whole story of what had transpired there come out. 'I love it. We should bury this guy in the snow and take our time about getting this place sorted out.'

'School's still in so I don't have to hurry home.'

It took them two weeks. They did everything slowly and meticulously because they wanted to get back to as close to their normal weight or heavier if possible. There was still plenty of unburned stores even if some of it tasted smoky or had changed consistency. They had to spend some fuel to travel out on the machines to bring in enough wood for all of the camp to burn. The wood lined tents they pulled apart. They were able use a small solar power emergency unit that the operations used to ensure power to the communications system to charge up the three power blocks they found which would be used for Jake's phone when they were travelling because it kept a charge.

The southerner on ice ended up with some blood and fibres from the other men's jackets on his body and some skin from each under his nails or rubbed up against him. They cut a new pike like one that killed Davey, drove into Davey for a second time and rubbed the southerner's hands all over it. They'd take it with them.

Another thing was going to be found on the person of the Southerner. When they had come to deal with the bodies of Doc, Claude and the South African.

'On this occasion I am thinking what you're thinking.' Jake replied simply when she looked at him while standing next to Doc and Claude.

They got more glass eyes and used the Southerners hand to get the used ones out of Kirk and Bertram, and also put the new one's in Claude, Doc, the South African and what was left of Davey, and then take them out again. All these were put in a plastic bag in the culprits pocket.

'That man was one sick serial killer who had…like a …'

'Signature.'

'That's it. Nasty. Lucky you took care of him or who knows what would have happened.'

'We would have had glass eyes of our own. And I bet he'd be so nasty he'd give us crap ones. Not the one's we, I mean he, put so much thought into for everyone else.'

'What a bastard. Damn him to hell is what I think.' She looked at Jake. Excited about a possibility. 'Dancing Bear Guy.' They wore their alter ego skins constantly. 'Imagine how cool it would be…if we ever get back…to be watching TV together and a program comes on about this weird story in Northern Canada where this evil man goes on a killing rampage and replaces the eyes of the people in an illegal animal killing operation with glass ones.'

Jake was nodding thoughtfully. 'You know, as far as the people making the program know, they'd be quite right to suggest he may have done it before he killed them.'

'Whoa. I didn't realise what kind of perverted murdering crazed killer we were dealing with.' The were standing by the body putting DNA on it so Reece gave it a kick. 'Before they even died. What kind of a twisted freak are you man.'

It had taken a long time to get the wood in and everything in place.

One body was treated with special reverence. Jake knew quite a bit about dogs and Reece knew she didn't like killing them.

Clive was slid off the pike he'd been skewered on and placed on the pile of deer skins in the merchandise hut when it went up. Reece stroked his fur. 'Thanks for not catching me Clive. Sounds like you'd be the only one who would have been worth leaving with us.' Fred and Ginger were interred on lower piles of skins. And the wolf with the burned hide on top of the remains of his kind.

All the human bodies were put in the barracks room for which they used up most of the woodpile in the camp. 'I want to pick the tune for this if it's okay Jake.'

The fact they were going to dance while everything burned had not been something Jake anticipated.

They lit up the fire.

'It was going to be a song called Firestarter but I decided I liked another song by the same band. It's call Breathe by Prodigy.'

'Don't think I know that band. Have we listened to their stuff before.'

'There wasn't the right occasion until now Jake. And now is the right occasion. Trust me. This is the song we gotta dance to while this…evil place burns to the ground.'

Jake got it. Burning the place felt good in some ways. Sad in others. The three dogs and the wolf were collateral damage they regretted. The people they had not a shred of guilt about. The fact so many animals would now not end up on a floor or hanging from a wall meant that as they camp burned they played the song again and danced around with an abandon neither of them thought they would ever feel. Especially if someone else was around.

The camp was in ruins. Every structure was burned to ashes.

Days of thought and care had gone into what clothes they would take, trying on what was always top-quality winter wear. They had boots, two layers of thermals and one in their packs, a shirt and a jacket each. Trousers and snow pants, balaclava, beanies, gloves and heavy mittens. They took a gun each, packs full of food, plus several things they decided the Southerner might like to have in addition to a zipped up pocket full of used glass eyeballs along with half a dozen real ones floating around in Kirk's bottle of scotch. The man was kept buried in a heavy layer of snow until they were ready to leave.

Looking at the ruins they stood in the quiet for a while. 'I'm going to miss this place.' Said Jake.

'We had some good times here. Be nice to get this ride on the...damn...the drive over snow contraption over with and get back to our journey.' Jake got the impressions that riding on a snowmobile was close to cheating for Reece. But necessary. They we still going to earn the feeling of achievement at the end of it.

Jake breathed deeply and smiled. 'And spring's just around the corner.'

There was so much weight on the machine, even having tipped every drop out of the big fuel tank, the labouring motor chewed through the fuel faster than expected. They also needed to burn more fuel and time than expected scouting trying to find a location to send the whole arrangement over a cliff. The fuel was dangerously low with no sign of a suitable cliff. They spent three days walking out from where they'd made a nice camp, the Southerner buried in deep snow as he'd been every night. Strangely they didn't get anxious about it.

They talked about their circumstances and decided it was essential they were not going to get dragged into something that; Wasn't anything to do with us. As Reece characterised it. They found somewhere well suited eventually. It was a day's walk north by northeast but they didn't mind.

They pointed the machine over the cliff at an angle and had it idling. The Southerner, by now quite unprepossessing, was put in the rider position.

Jake stood back and smiled. 'I got to throw the rock so Wolf Girl, you can do the honours with his driving mishap. She put her gloved hand over his and revved the machine, running with it to the cliff edge. She pretended she didn't need it, but she was grateful to Jake for holding onto her by the shoulder. A close call gave her an excellent view of the machine cartwheeling over itself a few times, satisfyingly throwing the rider and the cargo in all directions.

Jake smiled. He wasn't always certain. But this time he was. 'Are you thinking what I'm thinking.'

'This calls for a tune and some apex predator moves.' Neither could imagine themselves laughing and dancing with anyone else the way they did in the frozen wastes of Canada. Especially when they'd just sent the Glass Eyeball serial killer to his well-deserved demise.

Once they were back walking for an hour it started to snow. 'They'll probably never even find that guy. After all the hard work we put into catching that sick…I can't even think of a word for someone who would do that stuff.'

'Hopefully the whole arrangement gets overgrown and forgotten.'

They started walking again the next day and soon got into a rhythm. Though now it was different. They had plenty of rice, a few condiments and could use the guns if rock throwing didn't turn up anything. They still tried it though until they ran out of meat They continued their navigation through the thousands of lakes throughout that part of the country and were no longer frustrated at trying to guess the best route or concerned about the ice breaking under them when they chanced a crossing. They decided that based on the rate the three external batteries drained they would have a tune in the morning and one around the fire at night.

After two weeks of walking the signs of spring were emerging. They were surprised how quickly things began to melt away and the green shoots emerged on the ground and some of the bushes and trees. 'It's nice to see some springtime. I was worried we'd get back too soon.' It was getting decidedly warmer. Half of their stores had been consumed and the space was now taken up with clothing. Since they had begun they had never once left a shred of clothing unworn so it was strange to be carrying around top quality cold weather gear.

They were always wearing their skins. They both knew the opportunities to be Wolf Girl and Dancing Bear Guy might be thin on the ground when they got back. As the thaw continued, one morning they were walking along in a state they had both eventually found easy to fall into. Reece called it 'Nothing on my Mind' time. They realised in their former lives they both usually had something on their mind. Even Jake, who, though he lived on a ranch, there was always information flowing in and too a degree, needing to flow out. Or at the very least what was coming in needed to be processed.

A large male Grizzly bear emerged, apparently from nowhere and stood at full height only half a dozen paces away. They snapped out of that zone and were immediately focused. They had seen bears at a distance and moved away quietly. The closest they'd been was when one was gorging itself on salmon. Heading into winter the bears were focused on eating, and it seemed there was plenty for them to eat. They were asleep in winter, so this was the first they'd seen for months. And it was a bad time to run across one. Because they wake up hungry, and, based on the mood projected by this bear, irritable.

'Haven't come across many bears.' Said Jake quietly. 'I've heard you're supposed to stand still. If you run. Well...they can run faster and once they start chasing you...it probably makes them figure they might as well stop you. And...a bear like this could do a lot of damage before you put it down with bullets.'

This all came over as slightly odd from a man in a grizzly bear skin. Reece believed they were simply two pieces of meat within striking distance. Jake's gun was over his shoulder. Reece liked to carry hers in front, her Staff of Justice tied to her pack. They had started to come across deer, elk and a couple of Moose. She would either bear up on them while standing or if there was time they would crouch, and then lay down and take aim with a very expensive gun with a top end scope. She would aim where Jake taught her, get the animal in the sights and say. 'BAM.' As the animal ran away, or in the case of the moose look on at her disdainfully she'd say. 'Thanks for being so beautiful for us.' Small animals were hunted when they were big enough so they could eat the whole animal including carrying some of the meat.

This giant bear was aggressive. It may have been an unpleasant bear even compared to the larger bear cohort.

To Reece it was like a mosquito. Compassion and concern for a species vanish when they were poised to kill you. Or even create a little discomfort. Reece lifted the rifle. She knew the sights were useless at this range. She took one shot. The creature was unhappy for a half a minute then fell backward. It had been shot clean through the eye.

All Jake could say was. 'Wow.'

'I didn't like the way that bear was looking at you. I was concerned what would happen to my delicate young mind if I had to witness any…unwelcome advances.'

Jake went and inspected the shot. 'That is one big pile of bear and one magnificent shot.' He was sincerely impressed. Reece tried to move past what had been unquestionably a large serving of luck. Which in her mind; they damn well deserved.

'It's gonna take some time for us to eat that much bear.'

'With it getting warm like this I think we'll only be able to do only so much. I suspect the other bears will be grateful to you to have removed this individual from the bear community.'

'I found him rude and unpleasant to be honest.'

'Hence you killed him. Which I hope you can appreciate I am deeply grateful for.'

'Yeah I knew you couldn't do it because it's like a totem thing for you now. You'll have to take care of a rude and unpleasant wolf.'

'Guess it's time to cut off some lumps as big as we can carry and find a nice place to camp. Never eaten bear so this is out lucky day.'

'Again.'

'Exactly.'

Stopping for two days to eat and dry bear meat brought back what were now good memories of stopping to dry out most of Boo Boo and the Elk the wolves killed for them. As well as lots of other times they'd stopped to take their fill and dry out smaller game.

Two weeks later they were camped on a rise with a big fire. They had warm clothes now, so they didn't need to set trees alight. Secretly neither wanted to attract attention. They wanted to arrive on their own terms. Jake looked up from his phone. 'Three bars.'

Reece hadn't been quite ready for that. 'Whoa. Three bars. Yeah. Hey. How about that.' Her voice trailed off.

'Yeah.' Replied Jake. Neither were filled with the rush of joy they might have had when they were stumbling, exhausted, cold and starving. It felt strange to be looking at an app. He was looking at a map of where they were. Reece was standing next to him. She said what he was thinking.

'We're a blue dot again.'

He laughed. 'Yeah. And look at that. There's a mine fifty miles behind us, and off out to the west. The road to it is ten miles or so the other side of that lake we went around.'

Reece held out her hand. For all they'd been through it was hard for her to watch the plodding way Jake interfaced with the device. For his part he had never seen a device interrogated so quickly. The experience had sharpened Reece's mind and calmed his. People who knew him assumed he had one like that already. But they were wrong.

He could see what the focus of her searching was soon enough. She had searched a local news site. The authorities had found the camp. There had been some unusual flare ups captured by one of the myriads of satellites that now scrutinised everyone's backyard. 'Got there a week ago. Still haven't found that bad bad man.' She sat down on the log around the fire. They had a little tent but unless it was snowing they slept as they had since the first night.

Back to back. Curiously they didn't need to look out for wolves. They were animals that apparently either knew what a gun was or that the people carrying it weren't as afraid as they needed them to be.

They were sitting quietly. Reece was wrapped in Boo Boo even though it was warm by the fire. Jake was a little surprised she gave no hint she wanted to call anyone.

'Would have been nice to see more of the place in springtime.'

'Yeah.'

'If we walk out in a straight line, even when we ditch the clothes and guns…and…' She only then realised they had made a mistake. Though a natural one given they had been hungry for so long. '…we're so well fed and all.' She shrugged. 'And they didn't find the real killer.'

Jake realised that they could become entangled in something which, if interrogated closely, a detail told by one, which they hadn't concocted in detail yet, would only need not to fit with a detail from the other. He'd killed two people plus Hansen now that he thought of it, and Reece had taken five lives. Though it didn't feel that way. Even if self-defence was proven it could be a very long and unpleasant process all played out before a morbid public.

And then she said something surprising that made him realise there was more than one reason for her to be underwhelmed by a phone signal.

'We're going to do this again right?'

'Absolutely. There's trails that right up though the high county of the US and along the coast and…and right though other countries.'

'Yeah. Probably not for Wolf Girl and Dancing Bear Guy.'

'Who says we have to stay on the trials?'

Her voice was a little brighter. 'Yeah.'

He knew he'd need to help her with the next decision. She would be thinking of his desire to reach out to his friends, and especially the people who were on the ranch. 'I think we need to see a little bit more springtime.' He said. 'Maybe head towards that place we found and sheltered through the winter. Even if we have to go a good way east to get back to it. Might walk a little longer each day.' He might have said. 'And keep an eye on the news.' But she understood. She started searching satellite images and all kinds of web pages with old records, back country walking guides and topographic maps to the east and came up with half a dozen targets and took screen shots and various distances.

And also places further north which might be a probable location for the start of their tale.

They were up before sunrise and started walking. They were moving as fast as they ever had and were soon hungry. But were accustomed to it and they knew there was plenty of food. They would be eating very little of it and the wildlife went unmolested. They needed to lose condition. It was decided they were going to go on to have many adventures in the years to come and to do that they could not take the encumbrances of Russell Hansen or Kirk and his crew with them. It was fortunate they'd had enough signal to download maps and images because the direction they travelled in led them through areas with no signal. In two weeks they had covering ten times the distance they had in the dead of winter and on this leg of the journey eaten even less food.

Though they were shedding weight at a rapid pace walking ten hours a day over rough terrain, choosing to do it and knowing there was had plenty of food made it easier. The third place they visited was what they were looking for. Long ago it had once been someone's hunting cabin, possibly improved from a trapper's haunt from days gone by. It had a roof and four walls and the edge of a large lake a few hundred yards away.

The inside was covered with moss and with a few days of hard work it was liveable and after a few more it was clean. They spent hours catching fish, rabbits and rodents. Although they were sad at the waste they cooked them, took off the meat and buried the bones nearby, leaving parts of the fur and skin sprinkled around the cabin.

The story they would tell would need to explain how they got through the winter. It had required some internet searches on the night they had a signal to figure out a place within five hundred miles north of the cabin Russell could have landed his plane. There was nothing frozen over at that time of year so far south. They had walked through a lot of landscapes and picked one, where it might be possible to land a Grand Caravan, well known as a tough aircraft built for rugged landing conditions. Hansen had stranded them there, however with a cargo load of food and gear to see if they could survive and 'walk home'. As to why; they would say that as far as they could tell he'd gone insane. The plane was damaged on the landing, but he took off, barely, and they assumed he flew home.

The story which was decided on, was that they followed the advice to those lost in the wilderness, that they stayed where they were.

Some time was spent learning survival skills to make the food last, which included bags of rice, condiments as well as knives and plenty of warm clothing and a tent. By mid-way through autumn, when no one came, they assumed Hansen had succeeded in concealing what had happened to them and where they were. They decided they needed to walk out. However they had no idea how far they needed to go. They were fit and well and had full packs of food to carry out but after a month Reece injured her thigh, and they were concerned they would die of exposure if they kept going. They stayed in the tent for a week and then Jake scouted around and found the decrepit cabin. They sealed it, built a fire on the lake until it made a hole and lived on fish and rodents and a very low ration of the food they'd brought with them. Including meat from a caribou they'd chased a pack of wolves from. And they had the hide to prove it. Then at the end of winter when they planned to leave Jake got sick. Feverish and delirious. Reece was convinced he was going to die while they both starved. He gradually recovered. They went through the story together again and again so they started to believe it themselves, then would remind themselves that what they'd done was way more fun.

After saying this Reece would reflect and say. 'Are we bad people?' Then they'd laugh.

Halfway through the spring they walked towards a town that was two hundred miles away and climbed a large hill they believed would give them a nice view. Not of where they were going, but the wilderness they'd come from. There was a signal. They stopped and made camp and waited until they'd had their starvation ration, the sun had set and they were sitting around a small fire, eager to find out one piece of news. Reece's relief was palpable. 'The Glass Eye Killer' had been found trying to escape with valuable skins. Some from endangered species. It turned out he even had a backstory that featured some violence and robbery. And they'd found the old man who ran the ring of illegal hunters and taxidermists.

They did what they forgot to do last time and searched up their names. They, along with Russell were listed as missing presumed dead. There was speculation as to where the plane went down. Authorities assumed it was in the mountains along their flight path to San Diego though it was strange it wasn't found. The transponder had failed soon after the plane got on its approved flightpath. Pictures of her mother next to the most recent article encouraging the authorities to keep looking finally broke through to Reece. It helped make the call into which much planning had gone.

They would describe the power pack with them as something Reece already had and they had preserved for the day they thought they might get a signal.

Reece dialled the number and was surprised it was answered after only one tone. Jake could hear Tammy clearly. 'Jake. Jake is that you.'

'It's me mom. This is the first time we've had a signal.'

There was a rush of words.

'I'm okay. Or we're alive at least. It's been…hard.' Reece started crying which Jake found strange given they'd been though such difficult times, and it had been so infrequent. 'Did he tell you. Did he tell you he left us there with some food and camping stuff and took off.'

After listening for a time Reece said. 'We thought he flew home. We don't know where he went. He had it all planned. Left us with food and some warm clothes. He drugged us before we took off. We didn't even know where we were. We thought it was maybe Alaska. He was so angry. He said. See how you like each other now. Why would he do that to us mom. Why would he say something like that?'

Reece had departed from the script that had been carefully prepared. There were more words to which she responded.

'Could you come. Come and meet us and then we go to whoever we have to tell about what happened. We don't want ourselves to be a big…you know…focus. Jake and I want to go home to our normal lives.'

The next morning they were up early. They had their story as tight as they could ever get it. They were not going give an interview except in the company of Reece's mother in which Reece would be a shy and overwhelmed teenager and Jake would be a retiring rancher who, Reece insisted, had to be allowed to be seen by the world to have saved their lives because he was an 'outdoorsman'. They did as much of the last stretch as possible as Wolf Girl and Dancing Bear Guy until they found a good place to wrap everything they weren't supposed to have in a heavy tarp they brought from Kirk's camp. Once it was hidden Reece said. 'Are you thinking what I'm thinking.'

On this occasion Jake knew he had to decide. Had to specify what he thought they should do because she wouldn't. Fortunately it was obvious to him. 'When School finishes next year. A few days later we come and finish this journey. From right here where we're standing…to the ranch. Backcountry. Across the border where nobody will be looking. Wolf girl, Dancing Bear Guy and the Staff of Justice.' She smiled and nodded.

He looked at her with something more. This time he was thinking something beyond what she'd been thinking. 'We rest up for a spell. Then the Sierra Nevada's and on to San Diego.'

Because of Reece's nature and situation in life, there hadn't been that many uncomplicated smiles. Jake had seen most of those that were. 'Yeah. Mom can be there to meet us.'

Boo Boo had to come. The much-loved skin. Boo Boo was one of the partly true things in their story, although Boo Boo was brought down by the wolves in the 'fairytale' version of the trip.

As they were about to turn to walk the last few miles Reece's voice became serious.

She looked back at the landscape behind them. 'That asshole who flew us out there came to me less than a week out from the biggest event mom had on the books for the year and said he wanted to fly to San Diego for a family holiday the day before it. Said it was the only time he could do it. To me he was trying to drag me into a bullshit game he wanted to play with her, and I was a pawn. I was so sick of his shit I was honest with him. I told him from what I could tell I didn't have a family so how could it go on holiday. Told him I wasn't interested.'

'He came back later and told me that you wanted to come along and so I changed my mind, though I knew that likely wouldn't sit well with him. I told mom I would be very unhappy if she didn't do her event like she planned. Told her it would ruin my holiday if she even felt bad about it. I was expecting to have an awkward and lame pretend family holiday. Maybe it's because of what I said or maybe he'd already decided, but the asshole tried to crash us into a lake. He got it wrong. Instead of a lame family holiday I had the most kick ass adventure a girl could hope for.' She stopped and looked him in the eye. 'You gave me a present right before we got on that plane that I turned into a submarine.'

Jake nodded and pulled out a knife he never could have imagined would lose so much of its blade. He handed it to her.

'Who gave this to you Jake.'

He had never heard her call him that. Even as a child. 'My dad.'

'When did he give it to you.'

Jake swallowed. 'When I turned sixteen.'

'More similarities than differences right?' He was a little surprised he she knew his mind so well. 'Listen to me. We're going to see mom soon and there's going to be lots of crying and relief and stuff. And then you two were going to go off and have a talk and plan on sitting me down and give me a bunch of how comes and whys and wherefores and reasons why this happened and reasons why that didn't happen.'

She looked him in the eye with the intensity that had given Kirk pause. 'I don't ever want to hear any of that. From either of you. Never. You're always going to be Cowboy and I'm always going to be Reece, and I hope sometimes I'm going to get to be Wolf Girl and you'll be the Dancing Bear Guy. Everything else Cowboy…is bygones.' She held out her hand.

Reece had been the compass in his life that had made him try so hard to get to a place he'd always hoped to be. And now she had landed him right there. He reached out his hand with a smile.

'Bygones.'